As she walked ~~p~~ **arm. She stopped and faced him.**

"Where'd you go last year?" There was so much emotion present in his eyes. A mix of hurt, anger and something else...something much more primal simmered between them. Hunger.

Letting the chemistry between them rule would be a huge mistake and yet her feet were planted.

"We should get some sleep." The words sounded hollow even to her.

She couldn't.

Heat ricocheted between them as they stood this close. Where his fingers touched her forearm tingles of uncapped sexual energy pulsed.

"It's better for both of us if I don't say."

"Why? Because you plan to disappear again when it gets tough? Use those same places to hide?"

She turned her face away, not wanting to look at him. "Maybe."

"On our wedding day. Did you mean those vows or were they just empty words to you?"

She should lie. Tell him what he seemed to need to hear. That it was all fake and she'd never loved him.

She couldn't.

"Yes."

"Then why didn't you trust me enough to tell me the truth?" he asked.

CORNERED AT CHRISTMAS

USA TODAY Bestselling Author
BARB HAN

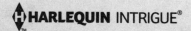

HARLEQUIN INTRIGUE®

All my love to Brandon, Jacob and Tori, my favorite people
in the world.

To Babe, my hero, for being my great love and my place to
call home.

To Jeff Amsden, for Phoenix.

ISBN-13: 978-1-335-60464-4

Cornered at Christmas

Copyright © 2019 by Barb Han

Recycling programs
for this product may
not exist in your area.

Printed in U.S.A.

USA TODAY bestselling author **Barb Han** lives in north Texas with her very own hero-worthy husband, three beautiful children, a spunky golden retriever/standard poodle mix and too many books in her to-read pile. In her downtime, she plays video games and spends much of her time on or around a basketball court. She loves interacting with readers and is grateful for their support. You can reach her at barbhan.com.

Books by Barb Han

Harlequin Intrigue

Rushing Creek Crime Spree

Cornered at Christmas

Crisis: Cattle Barge

Sudden Setup
Endangered Heiress
Texas Grit
Kidnapped at Christmas
Murder and Mistletoe
Bulletproof Christmas

Cattlemen Crime Club

Stockyard Snatching
Delivering Justice
One Tough Texan
Texas-Sized Trouble
Texas Witness
Texas Showdown

Harlequin Intrigue Noir

Atomic Beauty

Visit the Author Profile page at Harlequin.com.

CAST OF CHARACTERS

Lily Grable aka Kimberly Kent—This Kent bride faked her death to protect her new family.

Mitch Kent—The eldest Kent brother lost his wife after the birth of their twins. Or so he thought.

Randy Bristol—This shipping company owner might have gotten in over his head with the wrong people and put Lily's life in danger.

Paul Baxter—This well-known criminal is ruthless and will stop at nothing to make sure there's no trail linking him to his crimes.

Kenny "Tonto" Tonornato—This young guy needed a hand up. His desperation might just lead to murder.

Chapter One

The weather was warmer than usual for a late fall morning in North Texas, the heavy air loaded with the threat of a thunderstorm. Mitch Kent was gripping the handlebar of the double stroller so tightly as he stalked toward the medical plaza that his knuckles were turning white. Anger roared through him as reality sucker punched him. He'd already lost so much. A father twenty-three months ago. A wife less than that. The possibility of losing Rea, his infant daughter, gnawed away what was left of his gut.

Granted, all signs pointed toward positive news this visit for his younger and smaller twin. Life had taught Mitch how fast it could reverse and how devastating it could be when it took a wrong turn. He felt like he had about as much control as a sailboat in a hurricane. And that made him all kinds of frustrated. Mitch didn't go the helpless-victim route.

His cell buzzed in his pocket, breaking the pressure building between his shoulders that was threatening to crack him in half. He fished it out and checked the screen. It was Amber, his sister and the youngest of six Kent siblings.

"Wish I could be there with you, Mitch." She skipped over hellos.

"It's fine," he said probably a little too fast.

"You're not and you don't have to be," she countered, her voice strained. He appreciated the concern, just not the fuss.

"We talked about it last night when you called. You're needed at the ranch and I can handle this," he reassured her. He hoped she didn't pick up on the emptiness in those words.

There was a long pause.

"Are you sure you want to do this by yourself?" she finally asked. He didn't want to do any of it alone but life had detoured, leaving him to roll with the turns and try not to get sucked into the current.

"I haven't had two minutes of privacy since the twins were born," he said with a half laugh. That part was true enough and he tried to lighten the mood with humor. Anything to keep his thoughts from taking the headfirst dive that always left him wondering how he'd do any of this without Kimberly.

"You know what I mean." She was the last of his siblings to call before the twins' one-year checkup. Each of his brothers—Will, Devin, Nate and Jordan—had done their best to lift Mitch's mood. During the appointment, he'd learn if his younger twin, the little girl, was in the clear or headed for surgery. The thought of anyone cracking open her tiny body was a hot poker in his chest.

"I know you'd be here if you could, Amber. The ranch needs you more than I do." The Kent siblings had inherited their parents' North Texas cattle ranch nearly two years ago, following their father's death. Their mother had passed six months prior.

The one-hour drive into Fort Worth had been smooth and the twins had slept most of the way. But the two were wide-awake now and taking in the scenery as he pushed their stroller onto the center of the medical plaza. A maze of buildings surrounded them and there was a memorial fountain that was catching the twins' attention in the center of the complex. Mitch stopped in front of the three-story glass-walled structure attached to the hospital in the state-of-the-art building that contained the doctor his wife had handpicked for their babies.

"She's going to be okay, Mitch. You know that, right?" Amber said, and he could hear the concern in her voice even though she tried to mask it.

"There's every reason to hope based on the last couple of appointments," he responded. The last eleven months without Kimberly had been hell. Mitch Kent missed his wife. He missed the way her hair smelled like freshly cut lilies when she would curl into the crook of his arm every night in bed. He missed the feel of her warm body pressed to his, long into the night. The easy way they had with each other, talking until the sun came up. And he missed coming home to her smile every night after a long day of working his family's cattle ranch. Losing her had damn near shattered him.

First his mother, followed by his father. Then his wife. He'd lost so much.

Mitch realized he was still tightly gripping the stroller with his left hand. He flexed and released his fingers to get the blood flowing again.

"Those babies couldn't have asked for a better father." With five rough-and-tumble brothers, Amber was the emotional voice of the Kent brood.

"They need their mother." There were more times than Mitch could count that he'd wished his wife was still alive. They might have dated only a few months before tying the knot, but he'd fallen hard. When a man met the woman he was supposed to spend the rest of his life with, he knew it. Hers had been cut way too short. "I'm glad they have you."

"Good. Because I'm not going anywhere. Call me Super Aunt." He could tell she was getting emotional based on the change in her tone and the lame attempt at humor.

"Sounds like a plan." He went with it.

"And don't forget Amy." She was referring to their cousin. Amber and Amy were close in age, and both were mostly sweet with wild streaks that got them in trouble from time to time. Both had hearts of gold, and he couldn't have asked for better women to be in his twins' lives.

"Call or text the minute you get word." Amber made him promise.

"I will," he said before ending the call.

Mitch would learn today if his daughter, born two minutes after his son and almost two pounds lighter, was in the clear. In the best-case scenario, the small hole in the wall that separated the two lower chambers of Rea's heart was still too small to cause any serious damage, like overworking her heart and lungs or sending blood flowing in the wrong direction. Mitch blocked out another possibility. The one that involved a lot of medical jargon, some kind of fabric patch and cracking open the center of his baby girl's chest.

The appointment last month had gone off without a hitch. The doctor had said he was encouraged by what he heard when he listened to her chest. All signs were pointing toward good news. But doing any of this without his Kimberly seemed wrong. Then again everything that had happened in the past eleven months since her devastating car crash had been all wrong.

An all-consuming fist of guilt took another punch at him for not stopping her from walking out the door that day with her car keys in hand. For the sake of his children, he pushed the unproductive emotion aside. Reliving hell didn't ease the burns.

His courtship with Kimberly might've been a whirlwind but his feelings for his wife were anything but a passing storm. He'd known her barely two months before popping the question, which had surprised him even more than his siblings. They'd gone along with the wedding without protest after meeting Kimberly and seeing the two of them together. And they'd stood by his side on that cold rainy day when he'd first heard about the crash.

Mitch rubbed the scruff on his chin and blinked his blurry eyes, forcing back the barrage of thoughts racing through him. Letting his mind run wild wouldn't bring his wife back.

Exhaustion had thrown him off today. He gave himself a mental slap to shake off the bad mood.

He needed more caffeine.

Sleep and twins went together about as well as hot sauce and ice cream, and Mitch was beginning to feel the effects of being up for most of the night with the kiddos. Both were teething, which pretty much meant drippy chins.

The sounds of his daughter's babbling floated on top of the heavy fall air. He'd insisted on naming their little girl after her mother, but Kimberly had argued against it. They'd finally agreed on Andrea if she could go by Rea instead—Aaron and Andrea. Of course, he'd take back every disagreement if he could get back that last day with her and tell her to stay home instead of walking her out the door, handing her the car keys and telling her how much she needed a break.

Rea was growing into a talker. Mitch had no idea what the little tyke was saying, but that didn't stop his daughter from prattling on and on. Both he and Kimberly were quiet people, so he wasn't sure how his daughter had gotten the trait. Aaron was the silent one. He'd pick something up and examine it rather than chuck it across the room. Mitch had a babbler and a thinker.

Mitch thought about the labels he'd picked up in the past two years. Ranch owner. Husband. Father. *Widower.*

The worst part about being the latter—aside from the sobering fact that he'd lost the only woman he could ever love—was the cursed feeling that Kimberly was somehow still alive.

Granted, her body was never found. But Mitch's other cousin, Sheriff Zachary McWilliams, had assured him that there was no way she'd survived the accident. The car, *her* car, had been pulled out of the ravine with barely half a windshield. Based on estimates, she'd shot out of the driver's side like a cannon and ejected some twenty-five feet across the water before sinking. The official search had lasted six days. Flash floods and more severe storms had complicated the effort, and her body had most likely been swept away. Extra divers had volunteered to work on their days off once word had gotten around that Mitch Kent's wife had been involved in a terrible accident. But getting a late start because of worsening conditions had meant recovering a body was less likely.

He'd requested privacy from the media, which was something he was certain his wife would've wanted. Zach had also assured him that it would minimize the number of crackpots coming out of the woodwork, trying to get a piece of the Kent fortune. Mostly he'd done it for his wife. She'd insisted on staying out of the spotlight. The family attorney, Harley Durant, had kept the entire story limited to a blurb on the last page of the *Fort Worth Star Telegram*. Harley knew how to move mountains. He also knew how to keep a secret, and he had enough connections to back it up.

Since losing Dad and inheriting the cattle ranch with his five siblings two years ago, Mitch had been getting a good feel for running the place, and that was in large part due to Harley. So far Mitch was the only one living on the land full-time, but construction was planned or in process for the others to join him on the property with homes of their own.

It had been him and his wife living on the ranch up until now. Mitch still half expected her to walk through the front door.

He'd been told by a well-meaning aunt that he couldn't expect closure because her body had never been found. The same person had encouraged him to join a support group and find a way to move on. Mitch didn't especially believe in that mumbo jumbo. It was most likely the fact that Rea's eyes and thick black hair made her look more like her mother every day. Both twins reminded him of Kimberly. And maybe that was the reason he saw her everywhere.

Mitch pushed the babies toward the double glass doors of the three-story building attached to the east side of the hospital.

His cell buzzed in his pocket again, so he fished it out and checked the screen. Out of the corner of his eye, he caught sight of someone staring at him and a chill raced up his spine. Coming up on the anniversary of Kimberly's death must be playing tricks on him, because the woman was her height and had her figure, so his mind immediately snapped to thinking it could be her. Damn, he needed to get a grip.

Did he really think Kimberly would be at the plaza near the hospital and pediatrician's office? That was impossible. He'd buried Kimberly Kent at least mentally if not physically. Her grave was in the meadow she loved, not a hundred yards from the house, from her family.

"What's going on?" he asked his top cowhand, Lonnie Roark, aka Lone Star Lonnie.

"Found something near the base of Rushing Creek that I thought you might want to take a look at personally," Lone Star said.

"Okay. What will I see?" Mitch asked impatiently.

He wasn't frustrated with Lonnie; he was aggravated with himself for imagining his dead wife in the plaza.

Curiosity got the best of him, so he turned to get a better look at the woman. She shifted her purse to her other shoulder and he could've sworn her movements mimicked Kimberly's.

It couldn't be her, though. His wife had blue-black hair the color of a cloudless night sky that cascaded down her back. This woman had short, curly hair with so much bleach that it had turned white.

For a split second he locked gazes with her. She spun around, putting her back to him and tucking her chin to her chest. That was odd and it sent a cold ripple down his back. He strained to get a better look from this distance, but she'd moved next to a sculpture of some sort. He supposed it was modern art but he never did understand what that meant. The woman glanced back at him and his gut coiled.

Or maybe it wasn't that strange and he was just overly on edge. She sidestepped, breaking his line of sight as she blocked herself with the sculpture. What was Bleached-Blonde up to?

"It's one of the herd." Lone Star hesitated, which wasn't like him and set off a firework display of warning lights inside Mitch. This day was going to hell fast.

"What's going on?" Mitch tried to stifle his annoyance. He couldn't take his eyes off the partially blocked mystery woman. His need to get a closer look to prove she wasn't Kimberly set him off. If he knew what was best, he'd walk away. Leave it alone.

So why the hell couldn't he?

"One of the heifers must've caught hold of something and it tore one of her hooves off. Thing is I've searched everywhere within a fifty-foot radius and can't find the darn thing. What's left of her leg is a mess."

"You got an opinion on what could've happened?" Mitch didn't like the sound of this and it darkened his already somber mood.

"I'd be throwing spaghetti against the wall. There's no other sign of trouble and it looks like she died from bleeding out."

Mitch winced at the slow death that would've been for her. He bit back a curse. "Any tracks leading up to her?"

"Nothing I can see."

"You were right to call," he said on a sharp sigh. The stress of the day that had barely started already wore on him.

"I know you have enough on your plate this morning, boss." The people closest to Mitch knew about Rea's condition. Lone Star was in Mitch's inner circle. Even though Mitch was the boss, he and Lonnie were longtime friends. Mitch knew most folks in town, having grown up in Jacobstown, and he and Lonnie had been schoolmates.

"This was worth the interruption. Keep her right

where she is until I can get back. You were right about me wanting to see for myself. Do me a favor and keep everyone else out of the area until I can check it out." Mitch didn't like the sound of this one bit. It could involve anything from bored teens who were up to no good or acting on a dare to cultists, and Mitch wanted answers. If this was a prank gone wrong, he'd deal with it. Anger fisted his free hand. There was no excuse for making an animal suffer. "Thanks for the heads-up. Give me a call if you find any others. For now I'm assuming this is the only issue."

"Haven't found others but I have the boys counting heads," Lone Star Lonnie confirmed. "I'll keep my eyes peeled just in case."

"Let's keep the rest of the herd away from the area." Mitch figured it would be a good idea to keep them closer to the south-facing pasture.

He glanced up to see the woman had disappeared. Curiosity had him scanning the area, searching for her.

Out of the corner of his eye, he saw a streak of blond hair jutting out from the front of a hoodie. The woman wore jeans, tennis shoes and sunglasses. He did a double take to make sure it was the same person. Had she noticed that he'd been staring?

Of course she had; otherwise why put on the hoodie that had been tied around her waist? Mitch needed to turn around and get his tail in gear so he wouldn't be late for the doctor visit.

So why couldn't he force his boots to move?

Mitch rubbed his blurry eyes before ending the call with Lone Star. All kinds of scenarios ran through his mind about the mystery woman. Could Kimberly have survived the accident but had no idea who she was? Had someone saved her from the wreckage? Been keeping her all of this time?

No, someone would've put two and two together by now.

Lack of sleep wasn't doing great things for his brain. The woman couldn't be Kimberly. His wife was dead.

For whatever reason he couldn't take his eyes off her. Curiosity? Something else? Something more primal?

An ache formed in his chest. It was wishful thinking that had him wanting to get a closer look at the blonde. He'd already calculated the odds and knew this was a losing hand. Try getting his fool heart to listen to logic.

Mitch checked his watch. Technically he was ten minutes early.

Turning the stroller toward the mystery woman, he decided to double down on his bad luck. He scanned the area and noticed a pair of men on the opposite side of the plaza, standing with their faces angled toward her. She turned her head slightly toward the men and he could see her tense up. She took a step closer to a light pole and Mitch realized she was trying to block their line of sight.

Now Mitch's curiosity really skyrocketed.

Call it the cowboy code, but he needed to know that she would be okay. The blonde seemed to be in some kind of trouble, and he didn't like the looks of the two men wearing their jacket collars upturned, reflective sunglasses and ball caps. Very little of their faces were visible and his experience had taught him that law-abiding citizens didn't hide their faces in public. Nothing about either of them said they were law enforcement, so he assumed the blonde wasn't doing anything illegal.

One of the men moved enough to see around the light pole. He had his phone out, angled toward the blonde. Was he stalking her? Was he an ex? Someone she'd rejected? More thoughts along those lines crossed his mind, and none of them sat well.

Of course, a stalker would be alone. The guy standing next to the picture taker seemed just as interested in her, and didn't that jack up more of Mitch's danger radar? Were the men targeting her?

The blonde seemed to realize something was going on. Good for her. She wouldn't be an easy mark that way.

Once again his thoughts circled back to how familiar this woman seemed. Was there any chance his wife had survived the accident but lost her memory?

Could she have been walking around for the past eleven months with no idea who she was or where she came from?

It might be a stretch but he'd heard stranger things had happened.

Or did he want to see his wife again so badly that he was confusing her with a stranger? A woman who was similar in size and shape, who also seemed to be alone and in trouble? Was he grasping at any sign of hope?

There was only one way to find out.

Chapter Two

Kimberly's husband turned toward her and took a few steps in her direction. *No. No. No. Go back.*

Seeing her babies, their sweet faces, was so much harder than she'd thought it would be. The twins were one-year-old now and she'd known their first-year checkup would be around this time. It wasn't difficult to call the scheduler of the pediatrician she'd meticulously vetted to get the exact day and time.

Pain nearly crippled her but she fought against the tide of emotion. She couldn't lose control. There was too much at stake.

Life was about to spin out of control. *Again.* Seeing her twins one more time was a risk that Kimberly Kent—*correction*, Lily Grable—had had to take. The past eleven months had been excruciating, like living in a cave with no prayer of sunlight breaking through the darkness.

Life had taught Kimberly how to deal with loss early on. But nothing had prepared her for walking away from the only man she could ever love and the babies she'd only dreamed were possible. Happily-ever-after was for princesses, not orphans like Kimberly. And now she risked making all of that heartache count for nothing if Mitch recognized her. Or worse if the men watching her connected the dots to her family.

Panic seized her.

Let Mitch get a few steps closer and he would make a scene. She let herself take another look at him even though the grip around her heart from before tightened the minute she did.

Mitch looked even better than she remembered. At six foot four he'd always dwarfed her. His wide chest and ripples of muscles were visible underneath his Western shirt. Those muscled thighs… She could see wisps of his sandy-brown hair from the rim of his gray Stetson. The color of his hat would match the steel of his eyes.

Maybe she could play it cool and Mitch would stop. There was no way he could realize who she was with as much as she'd changed her appearance. *Right?* She looked at her husband from out of the corner of her eye and her stomach fell. He was too curious to give up, and that was bad.

He'd expose her, himself and the babies. She glanced toward the pair of men who'd found her. They'd seen her but had they pegged her? Did they know who she was? That was the big question.

Kimberly eased around the back of the sculpture, forcing her body to move away from Mitch when every muscle inside her wanted to run toward him instead. She breathed in the heavy Texas autumn air and tried to block out the memories of feeling safe in his arms. A storm was brewing and the humidity kicked up a few notches alongside her pulse.

Her heart pounded against her ribs at the thought she might be bringing the men who were chasing her right to her husband and children's doorstep. Whoever had killed her father and was now after her seemed ready to stop at nothing. The men wouldn't think twice about using her children or Mitch to draw her out. And even after two and a half years she had no idea what they wanted from her. All she knew was that her father had gotten himself into trouble. Beyond that she had no idea with whom or how. Her street smarts had kept her alive. She'd immediately changed her identity and gotten out of New Mexico.

But those creeps always seemed to catch up no matter how well she hid.

She'd had no choice but to disappear after giving birth, once the creeps had shown up in Jacobstown, Texas. She still had no idea what they wanted from her. Her father had left her a cryptic message to stay in the shadows until he cleaned up his mess hours before his death—a death that had been ruled an accident, but Kimberly knew better. There was no way her father would've drowned. He couldn't swim and was deathly afraid of the water, although he'd never admitted to that fear. The man had never once been out on a boat, so it made even less sense that he would've rented one, taken it out and then—what?—decided to jump off the side and swim for the first time in his life?

Guilt nipped at her. She'd known he was in trouble but she had been too involved in work at the small craft boutique and night school to stop to ask why. Her father had been acting strange for months, missing their dinner dates and not picking up his cell when she called. His behavior had been erratic and she could kick herself for not pressing him for details about why he was acting so weird. She'd honestly and naively believed that he'd tell her if something was really wrong. He'd always been her rock and she'd been able to count on him. Losing her foster mom to kidney disease had been hard on both of them. At the time she had thought that most of her dad's antics had to do with grief.

Looking back she should've seen the signs. Should've taken him more seriously. Should've been a better daughter to the man who'd taken her in when she was at her lowest point and saved her life.

"You're scaring me, Dad," she'd admitted when he'd asked her to get rid of her cell and use the new one he'd handed her.

"I'm being cautious," he'd defended. "Make your old man happy and use the phone."

"Only if you promise to tell me what this is about," she'd said.

"I will. Give me a couple of days to get it sorted out first," he'd promised.

"You're sure this isn't a big deal?" It had felt like one with the way he was acting.

"I owe someone a little money and they're blowing it out of proportion." He'd winked at her. "Nothing I can't handle. I just don't want you being bothered until I get this sorted out."

The only reason she'd left it at that was because he'd seemed embarrassed. She'd thought maybe he didn't want his creditor calling her, so she'd left it at face value.

Guilt was a face punch. If she'd pushed him for answers, he might still be alive.

When Deputy Talisman had all but accused her of foul play in order to inherit her father's business, she'd been defensive. It had become clear to her pretty quickly that she was going to be the target of his investigation. And then two men had busted into her apartment in the middle of the night. She'd barely managed to escape and had been on the run ever since.

Marrying Mitch had been done on a whim. The almost-immediate pregnancy had been a shock. And she would pay the price for those lapses in judgment for the rest of her life, which would be short if the creeps following her caught up to her.

A part of her wondered if this whole ordeal would ever be over. Could she come back to the life she'd loved with Mitch and the babies?

Reality said it would be impossible.

Her heart galloped at the sight of her husband

moving toward her out of the corner of her eye, along with her sweet babies, who turned one today. Birthdays were supposed to be happy events. But being this close without being able to touch her children felt like knife jabs to her chest.

Knowing that the twins would be at the office of the pediatrician she'd meticulously vetted prior to having those two little miracles had made it far too tempting. Going anywhere near Jacobstown, Texas, or the ranch was and had been off-limits. Those were lines she knew better than to cross. No matter how much she wanted—no, needed—to see her babies again, she couldn't risk bringing the creeps she'd been running from for an exhausting two and-a-half years to their doorstep. And then there was Mitch...

Seeing him again hurt.

Leaving a question mark in her husband's mind about her death wasn't ideal—a determined man could be dangerous. And part of her wished she could've confided in him, wished he could save her. She'd been close to confessing in the days before finding out she was pregnant. She'd known he would put his life at risk and she'd needed him to focus on protecting the twins.

How stupid had she been when she'd met him to think she could ever have a normal life? A normal life with kids and a man she loved, who loved her in return more than anything else?

That kind of love had been too powerful to turn her back on and had seduced her into thinking she could disappear into obscurity in the small town where she'd been hiding.

Mitch was everything a man should be to her—strong, virile…honest. Lying to him about her identity had been even more difficult because of that. Kimberly had been lying to herself for so long that she'd all but forgotten how to be truthful anymore. And maybe that's what had drawn her to the serious rancher with the steel-colored eyes.

Falling for Mitch Kent had been the easy part. She'd done that hard. Apparently she'd knocked a few screws loose when she'd made that tumble, because she'd landed in a fantasy that said if she kept a low profile, everything in her life would magically work out. But there were a few determined men who wanted to erase her presence. By the time she'd met Mitch, she'd already been running for six months.

A part of her wished—prayed—that he would forget all about her. The other part—the selfish part—couldn't go there even hypothetically. She wanted him to remember her, to love her.

"Kimberly," he said from behind her, and there was certainty in his voice instead of a question.

Certainty would kill them all.

A glance to the right said Mitch wasn't the only one about to close in on her. She felt like a mouse trapped in a maze.

There had to be something to use to create a distraction so she could get out of there. The air thinned, making it difficult to breathe.

A middle-aged woman wearing jeans and a light sweater walked toward her from the south with a black Lab on a leash. Kimberly bolted toward the woman and forced a smile.

"Can I pet your dog, ma'am?" she asked, pouring on the sweetness.

The woman beamed.

"Of course," she said as she went on about the dog's age and pedigree.

Kimberly dropped down to one knee before unhooking the leash in the bustling complex.

"I'm sorry," she said to the confused woman before popping to her feet. She shooed the dog. "Run!"

The black Lab darted toward the fountain as the woman gasped and then called after him.

Okay, Kimberly felt awful for doing that and wished there'd been another way to create a diversion. In the heat of the moment, that was all she could think of.

With another quick apology, Kimberly wheeled left and sprinted away from the pediatrician's building. A pair of heavy footsteps sounded from behind and she could tell by their rhythm that they were faster than her, racing closer and gaining ground.

At least Mitch would be stopped because of the stroller. Seeing those angelic round faces threatened to cripple her, but she couldn't afford to give in. She had to protect what was hers. Stuffing her feelings down deep helped her focus.

Kimberly's best chance to lose the pair of creeps

catching up to her was to get lost inside the hospital behind the pediatrician's office. She knew the area and that would give her an advantage. There would be armed security and the men following her wouldn't risk making themselves the center of attention by pulling something stupid. She hoped.

At least she could draw them away from Mitch and the babies. Kimberly sprinted around another building, trying to lose the men in the maze of buildings. Her thighs burned and her lungs were starting to wheeze.

The footsteps behind her stopped. Her worst fear seized her. Were the men circling back for Mitch?

Her breath caught and her heart screamed *no.*

How stupid and selfish had she been to come here? The past eleven months had been about taking calculated risks and watching her back at every turn. She'd just led those men practically to Mitch's doorstep. Kimberly bit back a few choice words, refusing to let negativity drag her under.

With the stroller, it would be impossible for Mitch to catch up to her. She'd cleared a few buildings and had crossed over to the front of the hospital, slowing her pace to a brisk walk as she entered through the automatic glass doors.

Activity buzzed all around her, and the modern lobby looked like a coffeehouse, with tables sprinkled around and folks on their laptops. The main difference was the fact that doctors and nurses cut across the open space, making their way to restricted-access areas.

Taking a chance, Kimberly checked behind her for the men. Nothing. Her heart took a dive.

Where were they?

MITCH FLEXED AND released his hands on the grip bar of the stroller. He'd scared a woman half to death by thinking she was his dead wife. Wasn't this turning into a banner day?

He wished he'd gotten a good look at Bleached-Blonde's face before she'd put her arm up to shield it and then disappeared in the commotion after a dog got loose from its owner.

Great. Now he could add scaring strangers to the already stressful morning he was having.

Thankfully the twins were clueless. Rea happily cooed and chatted, and Aaron took everything in while sucking on a pair of his fingers.

The men who'd been eyeing the Bleached-Blonde seemed to have given up on her. They'd returned to the plaza before heading toward the parking lot. It was probably Mitch's imagination that had him thinking those two were after her. He could add paranoia to his growing list of deficiencies.

The news from Lone Star Lonnie had thrown Mitch for a loop, on top of everything else he was dealing with, and maybe he was starting to crack. That was the only explanation for why he believed that he'd just seen his dead wife. She was on his mind even more than usual today. It was time to get back to reality, including getting his babies to their appointment.

Mitch pushed the stroller through the opened double doors and then took the elevator up to the third floor. He checked in and then waited.

A few minutes later he was ushered into the blue room to wait for the doctor and find out how much his life was about to change. Again.

Good news came from the pediatrician. Rea looked to be growing out of her heart defect. She'd have to continue to be monitored, which he'd expected, but the hole in her lower valve seemed to be closing on its own. Gratitude washed over Mitch, bringing a few stray tears to his eyes.

The drive from Fort Worth to Jacobstown gave him the chance to fill in his siblings and cousins, thanks to Bluetooth technology and his cell phone. Joyce, the twins' caregiver, met him on the driveway. She'd decorated the dining room with balloons and went to work serving lunch and cake to celebrate before taking the kiddos up for their naps.

Mitch had kissed both babies before picking up the fresh flowers he'd ordered and heading out the back door.

Joyce was a sweet woman in her late sixties who'd helped bring up Mitch, along with his siblings. She'd managed to wrangle six Kent children before retiring years ago but when she'd learned one of her "babies" was having babies, she'd insisted on returning to care for them.

Lucky for him, Kimberly had welcomed Joyce's help. The fact that she'd taken to the idea had caught him off guard at first. Kimberly had always been a private person. And that was where his luck had run out.

Sitting on the bench he'd carved out of solid wood beside the tallest oak on the property, he looked down at the marker. Kimberly Kent—loving wife and devoted mother.

She wasn't supposed to be buried there. His mind pointed out that she technically wasn't. It didn't matter. Kimberly Kent was gone.

He crossed his boots at the ankles.

When the twins were old enough, he'd bring them here to see their mother. He set the fresh flowers down—lilies. Her favorite. They reminded him of her, of her fresh-from-the-shower scent.

The wind started to pick up as a few more gray clouds rolled in, reflecting his somber mood. Rain was in the forecast, in the air, and it had been drier than a salt lick all week.

The feeling of being watched settled over him. Amber? One of his brothers? He scanned the meadow but saw nothing. Further proof that he was losing it.

The idea anyone could be in the meadow without his knowledge hit hard. Someone had been on the ranch undetected. The sheer amount of acreage owned by the Kent family made it impossible to monitor every inch. But still…

His gaze dropped to the plot of land in front of him.

"I saw you outside the pediatrician's office today," he said to the green grass over an empty grave. "Even though it couldn't have been you, I wanted her to be." He paused, choking back the emotion threatening to consume him—emotion that he'd successfully buried. "Rea's doctor visit was good. She's going to be just fine." Another pause to get his emotions in check. "I miss you, Kimberly."

Mitch cursed. Now he was talking to dirt.

He pushed up to stand as an empty feeling engulfed him, threatening to drag him under and toss him around before spitting him out again like a deadly riptide.

Pain made him feel alive after being hollow inside for months. The ache in his chest every time he took in air was the only reminder he was still breathing.

A prickly feeling ran up the back of his neck, like when someone said a cat walked over a grave.

Mitch didn't do emotions, so why the hell were his like a race car at full speed, careening out of control and toward the wall today? His baby sister's words from last year kept winding through his thoughts, drowning out logic and reason, the two things he was good at.

What if she's alive? What if she's still out there?

Mitch touched the grave marker, dragging his fingers across the smooth granite and into the grooves made by the letters of Kimberly's name.

And then he tucked his feelings down deep before texting Lone Star Lonnie that he was on his way to check out the heifer before it rained.

Walking away from his wife's grave was especially tough today. His thoughts were heavy as he made his way to the base of Rushing Creek, on the northeast side of the property.

Even though he'd prepared for the worst, the site still caught him off guard. Blood was everywhere. His heifer was on her right side in a pool of red on flat land. There was no sign of a trap that could've taken off her hoof and messed up her leg like that. She'd bled out and that would've been a slow death.

Anger roared through him as he thought about how much she'd suffered. It was inhumane to do this to an animal. Lone Star Lonnie had downplayed the situation with the heifer, Mitch thought as he stood over her.

Everything inside him felt as torn up and drained as the lifeless heifer next to him.

Whoever had done this would be brought to justice.

Chapter Three

The pitch-black night sky was a dark canopy overhead. Thick clouds smothered the moon, blocking out any possibility of light. Rain came down in sheets. The conditions were a problem. There'd be tracks. Kimberly couldn't afford to leave a trail or any sign she'd been there.

If the storm continued, there'd be no issue. Flash floods were common in this area of Texas and could wash away her hiking-boot prints. If the weather dried up, anyone could follow her based on the imprints she made.

She stepped lightly, careful to weave through the low-hanging branches rather than break them—again another way to track her movements. Being on the run had taught her to leave the smallest footprint possible. Leave a trace and someone would find her—the creeps following her had already proven that more than once. She'd racked her brain, thinking how they could've picked up her trail leading to the pediatrician's office earlier.

Kimberly cursed under her breath as tears threatened. How could she have been so careless? So stupid?

Guilt nearly impaled her.

She couldn't sit by and watch the only people she loved get hurt because of her. She had to make this right. She prayed that she could find the right words to convince Mitch to leave with the babies and disappear.

Seeing her alive would shock her husband. And he would hate her for what she'd done to him, to their family. Not that she could blame him. Sharp stabs of pain spiked through her, because she would feel the same way if the situation was reversed.

That wouldn't stop—couldn't stop—her from doing what she needed to do.

Being on the ranch brought back other memories. Memories that punched her in the stomach. Memories of being under this same sky on a starlit evening with Mitch's arms around her, feeling like she could slay her fears and stay right there for the rest of her life. Then there were all of those Sunday-morning breakfasts in bed after passionate nights.

They'd when she'd rented a cabin on Lake Orion. On her weekly trip into town for supplies was when she'd first seen him. She'd been at the lake for a couple of days already and had worn her hair down around her face, a light cotton T-shirt and a simple pair of jeans with tennis shoes.

Mitch had come up behind her while she stood in

line with her small cart filled with everything she'd
need for two weeks for a single person. He didn't
speak to her right away, but she turned to look at
him the minute she felt the strong male presence. It
seemed like every single woman in the place came
over to say hello while he stood in line behind Kimberly. Mitch was handsome—no question about
that—but he also had a sexual appeal that made
women blush when they spoke to him. The pitch
in their voices raised and it was so easy to tell they
were flirting.

Kimberly thought her eyes would roll into the
back of her head when one of the women nearly
knocked over the media stand while she compli-
mented his boots. There'd been so much bemuse-
ment in his voice—a deep voice that trailed down
the sensitive skin of her neck and wrapped around
her—when he thanked the woman that Kimberly
had almost laughed out loud. The ladies had been so
sickeningly sweet that Kimberly wanted to throw up.

Her reaction must've been written all over her
face when she turned to get another look at the all-
male presence stirring up all of the commotion behind her. Yeah, she'd been rubbernecking but she
couldn't help herself. She had only a couple of weeks
to be in town and she needed to see what all the fuss
was about.

The second she turned and got a good look, she
realized her mistake. Her cheeks flamed, her throat

dried and a thousand birds fluttered inside her chest, leaving her to wonder, *Who is this man?*

Her hand fell slack and she dropped her wallet, spilling change all over his boots, which actually were nice. If embarrassment could kill a person, she would've dropped dead on the spot. Lucky for her, it couldn't. And the tall, muscled cowboy had dropped down to help her collect her things.

He'd been gracious and generous and all of the things she figured a cowboy code would require. But when his fingers grazed her palm as he handed over her quarters and pennies, pure electricity shot through her. Her body hummed and based on the look in his steel-gray eyes when their gazes connected, he felt the current every bit as much.

After introducing himself, he'd asked if she would have dinner with him that night.

It took a few seconds for logic to kick in and for her to remember how dangerous that would be for both of them, but it did and she refused—albeit without conviction. She thanked him for helping her, turned and was grateful she was next in line. The cashier acknowledged her with a smile as she busied herself placing her items on the motorized belt. Inside, she concentrated on trying to breathe as the cashier ran her items across the scanner.

Kimberly's pulse raced and all she could think about was getting out of there and back to the privacy of the cabin on the lake. She fumbled for the right dollar amount. Using cash was another way to stay off the grid.

The handsome cowboy had followed her to the parking lot as she loaded groceries into the plastic container she'd fixed onto the back of the dirt bike she'd bought from a seventeen-year-old boy who went by the name Smash. Based on the condition of the dirt bike, he'd earned that nickname, but she didn't care. All she'd needed was reliable transportation to get her to and from the store and something she could use for a quick escape if the need arose.

Experience had taught her to be prepared for anything and especially the pair of creeps who always seemed to be one step behind.

"You sure about dinner?" he'd asked with the kind of smile that made women go weak at the knees as he held out a fistful of coins. She knew for sure because her legs almost gave.

It had most likely been that moment of hesitation—that too-quick smile—that had him showing up two days after she'd refused him in the lot.

The rain had been coming down in sheets on that day, too.

"What are you doing here?" she'd asked as she opened the door to find him standing on her porch, waterlogged and even more handsome than she remembered.

"I haven't stopped thinking about you for two days," he'd said, and her heart pounded so hard against her ribs, she thought they might crack. There he stood, with rain trailing down the brim of his gray Stetson. He wore a black V-neck T-shirt that, soaked with rain, outlined every one of his mass of muscles. "Tell me to leave and I will. I'll leave you alone. You have my word. Agree to have dinner with me and we can go anywhere you like."

As he stood there, with rain dripping from his tall, muscled physique, all of her willpower—and good sense—took a hike.

"Only if we stay here," she'd said. "We have to stay inside."

His face had broken into a wide smile—the same one that had seduced her willingly by the third night. And then less than two months later he'd proposed.

Tears sprang to her eyes at the memories. Walking away from Mitch Kent had been one of the most difficult things she'd ever done.

And setting foot in the house they'd once shared was going to be right up there.

MITCH RUBBED BLURRY eyes as he heard a noise come from another room for the second time. He glanced at the clock as he muttered a curse. The twins shouldn't be up for another few hours.

In a past life, he would've slept right through the small creak. Having babies had trained him to jump at the first noise. If he entered the room fast enough, sometimes he could solve the problem before the other woke up. Let it go even for a few seconds, and he'd be dealing with two fussy babies and not enough arms to hold them both. Joyce had volunteered to move into the guest room half a dozen times, but Mitch had refused every request. Her heart was in the right place; she wanted to make his life easier. But Kimberly wouldn't have wanted it that way. She might've agreed to receiving Joyce's help during the day, but she wouldn't want another person taking care of their babies overnight.

Another creak sounded and he was awake enough to hear it clearly now.

He threw off the covers and slid into the jeans on the chair next to his bed. This noise in the next room had nothing to do with the twins.

Was someone inside his house?

His hardwood floors creaked in exactly three places in the hallway. The first two had already made noise.

And now came the third. His adrenaline surged, flooding his body with heat.

Someone was walking toward his bedroom.

The twins' room was across the hall and a fleeting thought struck that someone was coming for them. But who could that be? And how in the hell did the person get past ranch security?

It took a minute for that to sink in.

Another thought struck that it could be one of his family members, but that couldn't be right, either. His brothers and sister would've called if there'd been an emergency. There was no way his cousins, Zach and Amy, would show in the middle of the night without calling. Those would be the only people who could get past security.

Mitch double-checked his cell in case he'd silenced his phone instead of switching it to vibrate. He thought about the heifer, and for a split second he thought the butchering might've been a warning.

The doorknob turned, so he jumped into action. Whoever thought they were going to get the best of him had another thing coming.

In two seconds he stood next to the door. It opened toward him, so it would shield him as the intruder stepped inside.

This probably wasn't the time to realize his shotgun was locked in a gun cabinet, a precaution he took for the sake of his children. Even if he could get to it, it wouldn't do any good. The shells were locked in a drawer.

As the door eased open, Mitch held his breath. He had his physical size, athletic conditioning and the element of surprise on his side, and that was about it. He had no idea what could be pushing through on the other side of that door.

In that moment he regretted not arming the alarm. He'd put one in, based on his wife's insistence, but never used it now that she was gone.

Another few seconds and he'd be ready to grab whoever crossed that threshold. And he hoped like hell it was only one person.

Mitch flexed and released his fingers. He was ready.

A smallish—at least in comparison to his size—

figure slipped inside. He took a step toward the intruder and grabbed whatever he could, wrapping his hands around the person's upper arms. The intruder seemed familiar but he dismissed the thought.

Until the person kicked where no man wanted a foot and he gulped for air. The intruder put their hands on top of his and then dropped to the floor, breaking his grip. This person had skills.

"Stop it and I won't hurt you," he warned through sharp intakes of air. He was still trying to regain his footing after taking a hit to the groin.

Before the intruder could scoot away completely, he had a fistful of shirt material. He took another knee in the same spot, ignoring the pain shooting up his abdomen and causing his gut to clench.

Fists flew at him until he wrangled the stranger's arms under control, but in pulling him or her close he ushered in a scent—lilies—and froze.

The intruder scooted out from underneath him.

"Whatever you do, don't turn on the light," the familiar voice warned through gasps.

"Who are you?" he asked but he already knew the answer—an answer that was a throat punch.

"It's me. Kimberly."

Chapter Four

Kimberly needed to find the right words to get her husba—Mitch motivated to get out of the house and Jacobstown until she was certain the men who'd found her had moved on. Thinking about him in terms of being her husband only crushed her heart more.

Instead she stood there, mute.

"My wife is dead," Mitch said out loud. His angry tone came off like he said the words more for himself than for her benefit. Either way, they scored a direct hit. Guilt was another punch.

All she could think to do was back away from him, slip past him and dart into the twins' nursery across the hall. She didn't flip on the light because her eyes had long ago adjusted to the darkness and she didn't want to wake the babies yet.

She knew that he followed her based on the tension she felt radiating from behind her.

Mitch's hand gripped her arm as she started toward the set of cribs nestled against the wall. Her heart nearly burst at the thought she would actually get to see them again. Hold them?

"Stop right there." Mitch's voice came out in a growl.

Reality slapped her in the face. He was about to kick her out. She jerked her arm out of his grasp and whirled around on him.

"I know what this must look like but trust me when I say you and the babies are in danger," she said in barely more than a whisper. "If we don't get out of here right now, a pair of men will show up. And that'll be bad news for everyone."

He stood there and stared at her like he was facing down a ghost. And he was. At least in his mind.

Mitch stilled and she could tell that she was getting through to him. Angry or not, he'd always been reasonable. Even though she could tell his armor was up and she'd never truly be able to break through it again, he considered what she was saying.

"Where have you been?" he finally ground out.

"Around." As far as answers went, it was awful. But it was also true. And there was no way she was telling him her locations. It would be too easy for him to predict where she went next.

Mitch stood in an athletic stance and crossed his arms over his solid bare chest.

"Why?" There was no sign of weakness in his voice when he asked the question. No sign of long nights without her. No sign of the hurt he must've felt. His tone was steady as steel now. *He* was steady as steel. The only thing that could melt steel was a temperature of 2,500 degrees Fahrenheit, and his glare felt at least that scorching.

He deserved an explanation. There was no time to go into details. She needed to get him to safety and then she could figure out the right words. Everything had careened out of control faster than an Indy driver staring down a wall after veering off course. The wall was coming. The crash was going to be devastating. The only question was how many of the pieces she could pick up afterward.

"Please say you'll come with me and bring the babies," she begged.

"You're supposed to be dead. Explain to me why you're alive and standing in front of me." His arms crossed tighter over his chest and there was so much anger in his eyes.

"I can't right now. But I promise—"

"Not good enough." He stood there, being a stubborn mule.

"Mitch. Come on. Just listen to me," she started, but he stopped her with a hand in the air.

Frustration seethed, pouring off him in waves.

"Forgive me, but I've been talking to a headstone for the past eleven months."

Those words were daggers and robbed her of breath.

"I buried your memory and as much of you as I could along with it," he continued, unblinking.

Wind blasted the window, rattling the casing. She

jumped and sucked in a sharp breath. "We need to go *now*."

"The kids need stability. Being here will give them that." His lips thinned. "Give me one reason I should take it away from them."

He wanted answers she couldn't give. But asking him to trust her at this point would be a slap in the face.

Reluctantly, she moved into the hallway, knowing full well he'd follow. Waking the twins would create a commotion and her heart would break if she heard them cry. She also couldn't risk them drawing attention or covering up the sound of someone breaking in. Words failed her and she wanted to scream. Panic gripped her like a vise, squeezing air from her lungs.

Mitch was so close on her heels, he almost ran into her when she stopped.

"People are after me and they'll use you and the twins to draw me out. I shouldn't have shown up at the doctor's office today," she admitted, both hands out in defense.

"That *was* you?" Recognition dawned with the admission but it didn't help with his anger.

"I'm sorry, Mitch. I truly am. I made a mistake but I can't change that now. You and the babies aren't safe here."

"Why not call the sheriff?" He shrugged. Suspicion laced his tone and she completely understood why he'd feel that way even though it hurt.

"Because in my case that will do more damage than good," she admitted. The night-light plugged into the socket in the hallway cast a warm glow on his chiseled features. Again she stared into eyes of suspicion and disbelief.

"I don't know what to tell you. Sounds like you got yourself into a mess of trouble." His words came out clipped.

"It's so much worse than that. I got *you* and the *babies* in a terrible fix. There's no way out but to run. I need you to believe me, Mitch." She stared into his eyes, which had hardened toward her. Was she even getting through? Based on his stern expression and closed-off stance, the answer was *no.*

This wasn't the time to back down. "I'm serious, Mitch. Please come with me and I'll explain everything once we're out of danger. Trust me when I say men could show up anytime and they'll outnumber you. They'll bring weapons." There were times when she felt like she would always be on the run. By the time she met Mitch, she'd been running for half a year. When the man who raised her had given her a throwaway phone and insisted she try to reach him only using the cell, she'd worried that he might be getting senile.

The first few calls had gone fine. As fine as they could be with him acting so strange. He'd mumbled about putting her in danger, but he never explained when she questioned him. She didn't put too much stock into what he said. She knew full well that he was a decent man. She played along while she tried to figure out the next move. Counseling? Support group? Her thoughts moved to questions like was it safe for him to be behind a wheel? And was it okay for him to live on his own and continue to run his business? Her worries quickly shifted from thinking about taking his car keys away to realizing something was really wrong when he didn't answer her calls. Days later, the deputy had found him. He'd drowned, which was highly unlikely for a man who never went near the water. And now the men who'd killed her father were after her.

But then again gloom had always followed Kimberly. Mitch had been a light against so much darkness. Falling for him had been so easy, so effortless. He was sunshine in a world that had become pitch-black.

It was selfish of her to want to hang on to the feeling of finally basking in the sun again, a feeling she hadn't experienced in so long.

A well of resolve sprang inside her. Loving him was exactly the reason she needed to buck up and be strong right now. She'd put Mitch and the babies in danger. So *she* would get them out.

A flash of light followed by a crack of thunder split the night air.

"What do those men want from you?" he finally asked, and she realized he must've seen them earlier.

"They must've followed me to the plaza. I hadn't seen them in a few days, so I thought I was in the clear. I'm sure they saw my reaction to you and put two and two together because they disappeared when I was so close. They've never done that before," she admitted.

"They won't get past security on the ranch. They don't know the place like you do," he started and then paused. A strange look crossed his features.

"What? What is it?"

"A heifer's hoof was cut off, butchered. Any chance your men would do something like that?" he asked, and it was a genuine question.

"Like a warning?" She was already shaking her head. "No. They'd use you or the babies to draw me out. You wouldn't see them coming."

Mitch stood there, all fire and frustration. More signs she was making progress with him.

"It also proves someone can get past security," she added for good measure.

When he didn't argue, she realized she was getting closer to his agreeing to cooperate.

"I promise this will all make sense soon. Just please come with me. I don't know how much time we have before they get here," she stated as plainly as she could. Seeing the man she would always love stirred up so many emotions inside her once again. Emotions she needed to keep in check for the sake of everyone she loved. In another time and place, the two of them could have shared something very special, very real.

Where was the reboot button when it came to life?

"Look. I don't know what you have going on or what game you're playing but your problems are not my problems anymore. That all stopped when you walked out on us," Mitch said through clenched teeth. For a split second he thought maybe his wife had been in a crash and survived but lost her memory or her mind.

All hope was decimated when he heard her speak. She knew who he was. She knew that they had children together, children she hadn't once thought to check on in the last year. Those were her choices. This woman's mind was as clear as water in a mason jar.

So he stood there, examining her. Anger boiled inside him at the fact that she stood in his home without an apology for what she'd put their children through by making them live the first year of their lives without a mother.

"My wife is buried on the west lawn at the entrance to her favorite place on the ranch, the meadow," he ground out, trying and failing to keep his voice at a whisper. He refused to believe that the woman he'd fallen in love with could be so heartless.

His words were intended to deliver a physical blow.

"I—I'm sorry for that, Mi—"

"Don't apologize to me. I got exactly what I deserved. But they didn't." He nodded toward the babies' room. "Those two didn't do anything wrong."

Kimberly stood there, her gaze scanning the area.

She looked scared and a little bit angry. As much as he didn't want to admit it, she also had that protective-mother look. The one that said nothing and no one would hurt her babies. And he couldn't ignore what she'd said. Someone had slipped past security and butchered one of his animals on his watch. Could they get to the babies, too?

Determination radiated off her five-foot-six-inch frame. Standing there, she was just as beautiful as he remembered. Dozens of times she'd slipped into his dreams. He'd imagine her right there next to him in bed. Or bounding through the house with that energy and light only she had.

Never once did he envision she'd return in the middle of the night with a warning. There were scenarios that had crossed his mind. The loss-of-memory one had always been prominent. Maybe because that would explain her leaving him behind, with his heart stomped on.

His dead wife standing in his hallway in the middle of the night, trying to convince him to go somewhere with him before she explained what the hell was going on, wasn't exactly topping the list of scenarios in which he'd dreamed of seeing her again.

"Please, Mitch. I know I don't deserve your trust. But believe it or not I'm here to help not hurt anyone," she pleaded one more time.

"You can't hurt me anymore. I don't care what happens to you." The words escaped before he could reel them in. It wasn't true. He did care for his kids' sake. They needed a mother. But what kind of mother disappeared? Or worse—faked her death? "Why'd you do it, Kimberly?"

"There was a reason I was so private and never wanted to be photographed or interviewed the entire time we were married, a good reason. Did you ever once think that there could've been another reason besides the flimsy excuses I gave that I just didn't like having my picture taken or that I was just a homebody?"

"What reason did I have to question you? Until today I had no idea what you were capable of. I still don't know who you are." The words had the effect he'd intended—sharp and direct—even though a twinge of guilt tried to worm its way into his heart. Mitch slammed the door on that emotion. He had nothing to feel guilty about. He wasn't the one who'd abandoned their family.

"I understand if you hate me but everything I did was out of love." She seemed to choke back a sob as determination set her features. "No one, not even you, can call me a bad mother. I put my children first."

"Here's a question…" Anger was rising like a volcano that was minutes from erupting. "Why have kids in the first place if you didn't want them?"

"Is that what you think?" Her strong facade was cracking deeper. Anger shot from her eyes, which he could see clearly now in the soft light of the hallway. She looked like she was about to spew a few choice words at him but then she must've thought twice because she blew out a breath and let her shoulders sag. Kimberly had never looked so defeated. But he meant what he said. He couldn't possibly have truly known her if she was capable of—what? Faking her own death? Ditching their family? Walking out on him without so much as a word?

"I cared."

"Actions are more important than empty words," he stated. She wasn't getting off this easily.

Another gust of wind blasted against the kids' window, and Kimberly looked like she was ready to jump out of her skin. It was clear to him that something had her spooked, but without any real answers—and she'd been dodging his questions so far—he couldn't make a decent decision. And then there were the men who had been after her earlier. He'd noticed their intent and it had brought out his protective instincts before he'd confirmed she was his supposedly dead wife.

Yet going with her on a whim seemed extreme.

"Tell me why you're running and who's after you." He decided to play along. During the time they had been together, he'd never picked up on a hint of her losing touch with reality. No matter what else he felt about her, he knew she wasn't the type for drugs or alcohol. So if she was sane and not under the influence of any substance, he probably should at least hear her out. His heart clenched at the sight of her, and being this close without answers or explanations caused his fists to tighten.

"I can't." Her gaze darted around like she expected someone to blast through a wall or window at any second.

"Why are you really here?" he asked. Surely it wasn't to save him and the twins from some unknown threat. That would mean she cared.

"I already said." She could be stubborn. He'd believed it to be sexy before. And, hell, it was now, too. Even though nothing in him wanted it to be.

"Are you sure this doesn't have anything to do with the heifer we found near the base of Rushing Creek?"

"No. These men wouldn't touch your livestock."

"Tell me who's after you." Maybe he could put the pieces together to see if there was a connection. Or maybe she could tell him something that would make the killing make sense.

"I can't." A look of something—such as frustration or fear—marred her beautiful features.

"Well, then we don't have anything else to talk about." He faced her down, not budging an inch.

"I leave here and they'll show." She glanced at the wrist on which she used to wear a watch, but there was nothing there. "It'll happen and you won't be prepared."

"You're not giving me anything to work with. I can't evaluate a threat if I don't know what it is." No way was he softening his stance. Of course he'd do anything to protect the little ones in the next room. And after her visit he planned to take extra precaution. But he wasn't convinced that leaving the ranch was in the twins' best interest.

"I'm being honest. I can't tell you who's after me or why," she said on a sharp sigh. It was more than she'd planned to say. He could tell by her tense body language.

"How do you know someone's targeting you then?"

"It has to do with Randy Bristol, my foster father, but that's all I know." Thunder clapped and it got her feet moving into the babies' room again. "I know you wouldn't put either of these two in harm's way, Mitch. Believe me when I say trouble is coming your way whether you choose to acknowledge it or not. That part's up to you, but I can't let them get to my babies."

"You lost rights to these two when you died," he fired back.

"It's pretty plain to see that I'm still here," she said.

"Not in the court's eyes," he shot back.

"Try and stop me," she dared to say.

"Take another step toward those cribs and I'll do just that. Then I'll call Zach." He referred to his cousin, the sheriff, to rattle her. "He'll arrest you, which is something you said you can't afford."

She issued a sharp grunt but stopped. "You wouldn't do that to me."

"Try me."

Chapter Five

Kimberly stared at Mitch. His set jaw and narrowed gaze challenged her. Her back was against the wall, because that look said he wasn't going anywhere until she confessed. The only progress she'd made so far was the fact that he was listening to her.

"Someone is trying to get rid of me. This is somehow related to my foster father, but I don't know how or why. He warned me, sort of cryptically right before he supposedly drowned but was really killed, and then the deputy who interviewed me strongly insinuated that I benefited the most from his death. That night someone came after me directly," Kimberly admitted, and it was like a huge weight lifted off her by being able to say those words out loud.

He looked at her like she was crazy. She couldn't exactly blame him.

"I never knew you were in the system." He paused a minute as though to let his brain click puzzle pieces into place. "You said your parents died when you were a teenager, and you had to spend high school living with a sick aunt who'd since passed away."

She shot him a look. "I'm sorry that I lied before. He is the only father I've known. It wouldn't have helped if I'd told you the truth."

"How can you say that?" he shot back. "It seems to me that it matters a whole helluva lot that I had no idea who my wife really was and now my life is in danger."

How stupid had she been to think she could pull off a marriage and family when the creeps were never far behind? Granted she hadn't known she was marrying one of the wealthiest and most eligible bachelors in Texas at the time. His downplayed clothing, calloused hands and rugged good looks made him seem like a salt-of-the-earth type, a cowboy and not a wealthy ranch owner.

"You weren't exactly honest with me, either," she fired back. She'd been seduced by the idea that she could live on a ranch in a bunkhouse and be perfectly happy for the rest of her life.

"I thought you knew who I was," he defended.

It was her turn to balk because she was pretty damn sure he'd enjoyed meeting someone who didn't have designs on him for his family ties. "And Christmas comes in June."

Mitch stood there for what felt like half an hour but was probably less than a couple of minutes. An inappropriate shiver raced down her arms as his gaze intensified on her. The hint of appreciation in his honest gray eyes made her want things she knew better than to consider.

"You better plan on filling me in as soon as we're settled." His tone was cold enough to make her shiver. She rubbed her arms to hide her physical reaction to him—one minute hot and then the next so cold. There was more to it than she was ready to admit to herself, because thoughts of his hands doing other things to her crept into her mind. Those were useless. He was agreeing to go with her, and that's all she needed for now.

"Fine. But we need to go. They can't be far behind me and we've wasted enough time talking already. If we don't get out of here soon, it could be too late." It was her turn to fold her arms and dare him not to believe her.

He nodded.

"I'll pack up the twins." She moved to the diaper bags she'd seen sitting on top of the dresser.

"You can't. You don't know what they need." His words stabbed her in the way that hard truths often hurt. Hard truths like the fact that a dark cloud had always followed her. Hard truths like the fact that everyone she'd ever cared about hated her or was dead. Hard truths like the fact that she would never live a normal life.

"How do you know these people are after you?" He was stalling. He wasn't naive or slow. He had to know the men from this morning were hunting her.

A flash of light was followed by a crack of thunder that rattled the windows.

"I'll explain later. We gotta go *now. Please, Mitch.*" She could set her pride aside and beg for the sake of her children.

On an exhale, Mitch moved to the set of cribs.

If seeing him again was already a knife to the center of her chest, watching the normally rough-around-the-edges cowboy soften his stance as he picked up one of the twins nearly did her in. But then again Mitch had always been that perfect blend of raw masculinity and gentleness. His hands were rough as they roamed her body but she liked it that way. His hands might be rough but his touch was anything but. Thinking about all of the sensations those hands had brought about so easily sent a sensual shiver racing up her spine, tingling her nerve endings.

But her heart fell when she got a good look at her daughter's face from over his shoulder. Tears sprang to her eyes at seeing her. *Rea.* Such a beautiful baby with a round, angelic face topped off by thick curly black hair. Kimberly knew this was going to hurt. Seeing her daughter stung so much more than she thought. She was reminded of everything she'd missed. Her entire body ached.

What had she expected?

The changes in her daughter from a one-month-old infant to a one-year-old baby were staggering, and her breath caught.

"She's so big," Kimberly said so quietly that she didn't think Mitch had heard until she caught a slight nod.

"The trick is to wake her and get her changed before her brother opens his eyes." He walked over to a changing table, cradling the half-asleep baby against his bare chest. If there was something sexier than that image, Kimberly had never seen it. A dozen butterflies fluttered in her stomach. For a split second it occurred to her that the man holding that baby was *her* husband, or at least he *had* been.

As it was, Mitch wanted nothing to do with her. He was entertaining her by going along with her pleas. It was easy to see that he would never trust her again. Mitch was an honest and decent man. He didn't deserve what she'd done to him. Blaming their whirlwind affair on letting her emotions get carried away wasn't fair.

Kimberly had messed up big-time. She would pay the price for the rest of her life for that slip. Since she deserved every bit of misery that came her way, she wouldn't fight Mitch or try to convince him that she was there because she cared. And she sure as hell wouldn't let her eyes linger on the lines of his muscled back or his arm muscles while they bulged and released as he lifted their daughter and gently placed her on the changing table. Seeing him so capable with their child stirred her heart in painful ways.

Digging deep to muster whatever courage and self-discipline she had left, Kimberly forced her gaze away. Being around Mitch was exhausting. Emotions were more exhausting than anything she'd ever done physically. She'd been a runner in high school. She had no idea the same term would define her life now. Running had been an outlet for her pain. Workouts had started at five o'clock in the morning and she'd trained on her own after school sometimes, running to her job across town. At night she barely had enough energy to get through a shower before dropping into bed.

She thought about the charms she'd given her babies and moved to the top drawer of Aaron's dresser.

"What are you looking for?" Mitch asked as she dug her hand around in the last place she remembered placing Aaron's pair of silver running shoes.

It must've dawned on Mitch, because a beat later he said, "The box is on top of the dresser."

She looked up, not ready to admit how frantic she'd been fearing that he'd tossed it, along with any other memory of her. "If it had been a snake, it would've bitten me."

How many times had Mitch delivered that line to her when she'd been looking for something she'd misplaced?

"Sometimes it's hardest to see what's right under your nose," he stated. "Rea's is in the same place on her dresser."

She located both and placed one in each diaper bag.

"I'm sure I can figure out what else needs to be

packed. All babies need diapers and wipes," she said in a low voice.

Before Mitch could warn her to be quiet again, the other twin stirred. Based on the sound of the wail Aaron unleashed, he had a healthy set of lungs.

Kimberly didn't debate her actions. Mothering instincts kicked in, causing her to rush to his side and scoop him into her arms. His eyes were closed as he belted out another cry. The sound nearly brought her to her knees. She hoped that maybe he would realize his mother was holding him. Her body softened, a physical reaction to holding her son that she remembered from when he was first born. He was heavy now.

For a split second her world—which had been tipped on its axis for eleven long months without her family—righted itself. There was something magical about being in the same room with Mitch and the twins, like she was a whole person again after having her soul splintered into a thousand flecks of dust.

She nearly crumbled, as her legs felt almost rubberlike, at the thought of leaving them again. A tear escaped as she stood there, doing what she thought would never be possible again, holding her child.

Before she could get too comfortable, Mitch was there, taking their son from her.

Kimberly was so lost in the moment, she hadn't realized that Mitch had placed their daughter in a carrier that hummed with vibration.

Her arms felt so cold the minute the warm baby was plucked from them.

"I can take it from here," Mitch said, clearly uncomfortable with her holding their child. But he couldn't hold both of the twins every time. At some point he was going to have to let her help.

He had a territorial look that she knew better than to argue with at the moment.

Getting to hold her child, even for a few seconds, was so much more than she'd expected to experience after her disappearance. A selfish part of her was glad she had come back. But the feeling was quickly obliterated by the fact that doing so had just put her family in danger. The reason she'd taken off in the first place was moot. All that suffering for naught if she brought the threat to their doorstep. She could only pray that she was overreacting. That the creeps chasing her hadn't put two and two together.

What are the odds? an annoying little voice in the back of her mind asked.

Pretty damn slim.

A bolt of lightning lit the room, and the sharp crack of thunder that followed said the storm was directly overhead.

Kimberly bolted into action, moving to the set of diaper bags on the dresser next to the door and grabbing a few. She rummaged through drawers, looking for clothing, and then crammed a few items in each bag.

"You know security will stop anyone from driving onto the property," Mitch stated, eyeing her as his hands worked on the diaper.

"These people won't exactly drive up to the window and ask permission."

And when another bolt of lightning crossed the sky with the accompanying crack of thunder, she added, "We have to go *now*."

MITCH WAS STILL second-guessing his decision to load up the twins in the middle of the night and take off to nowhere with his supposed-to-be-dead wife.

Kimberly was alive. The thought hadn't really sunk in, and shock was most likely to blame.

Even so, here they were on the road with the twins.

"I need coffee," he said, pulling his SUV into the gas station on Route 25. So far they'd left the ranch without incident, despite Kimberly's dire warnings. If he didn't know her better, he'd think she was crazy. He also remembered seeing the men in the plaza who'd set his radar on edge and knew she was being honest when she said he and the twins were in danger.

Sitting in the front of the SUV, her stress level was high. Tension radiated from her. When they were married, he knew exactly what to do when she was anxious or upset. Now it hardly seemed appropriate to think about how to ease her tension. Her paranoia during their marriage made a whole lot more sense now. He didn't classify it as such while they were hitched. Things had changed.

She didn't argue but her gaze darted around the parking lot.

"You stay in the vehicle with the twins." He hesitated for a split second, but reality said she wouldn't do anything to hurt herself or the babies. If there was one thing he knew for certain about his wife—correction, about Kimberly—it was that she loved those angels sleeping in the back seat.

Car rides had been his saving grace in the early months following losing his wife.

He pushed open the driver's-side door and tried to shake the thought. Kimberly was alive. How many times had he prayed this scenario was actually true? Too many to count.

Now that it was true, there was so much confusion rattling around in his brain. Another reason he needed the caffeine boost. A small part of him wanted to believe he was still asleep, dreaming that his wife had returned. He'd had plenty of those nights in which he'd wake with a start, half expecting her to be right beside him. The smell of her shampoo—lilies—filling his lungs as he took a deep breath.

Kimberly, his wife, would forever be dead to him.

He opened the glass door leading into the gas station that doubled as a convenience store. This place had everything—and he meant *everything*—a traveler could possibly need or want, with enough cashiers to ensure no one wasted valuable road time waiting in line. The walls were covered, from the ceiling to the floor, with everything from bags of assorted nuts to sunflower seeds.

Mitch scanned the room and locked on to the coffee machine.

There were enough vehicles coming and going outside that his SUV would blend right in with the traffic and Kimberly would be safe. Changing his primary vehicle had been his wife's idea. He'd driven the same truck for most of his life, until the twins were born. Since their arrival, he needed more cab room, so driving a bigger vehicle made sense. He couldn't part with his F-150, though. It sat in his garage, reminding him of a time before life was filled with diaper bags and strollers. He wouldn't change any of it, though. Except the part about being betrayed by the person he thought had loved him.

Mitch needed caffeine. He made a beeline to the coffee machine. He wasn't the kind of guy who got really wrapped up in emotions. Being a cattle rancher was simple. Take care of the animals, and they'll return the favor.

So being anywhere near the woman sitting in his SUV brought another bout of anger flooding through him because her presence confused the hell out of him. He didn't want to feel anything for her, and yet she stirred a feeling in his chest that he'd buried deep down when he'd buried her.

He was so distracted by his thought that he overfilled his cup with black coffee, causing it to spill over onto his hand. Nothing woke a person up like burning-hot coffee on exposed skin.

Mitch shook it off, poured a little out and placed a plastic lid on his cup. He poured a second cup and pocketed a couple of packets of sugar and creamer for Kimberly. He paid and quickly took a sip of the hot liquid meant for him. It burned going down his throat in the best way possible.

Back at the SUV, Kimberly rolled down her window so he could hand her one of the cups. He gave her the condiments next, frustrated that he remembered in such detail the way she took her coffee. Two packets of sugar. One and a half packets of creamer. She stirred twice and then dipped the stirrer into her mouth to get the first taste. That was generally followed by a sigh of pleasure when she got it just right or a frown when the balance of flavor was off. Mitch liked his coffee strong and black; he didn't need any fancy fixings.

He took another sip as he rounded the front of his vehicle. His gaze stopped on a white sedan pulling in from the east entrance. It was the middle of the night but this place was hopping.

The sedan slowed to almost a crawl and an uneasy feeling settled over Mitch. What was this guy doing?

He tucked his chin to his chest and climbed into the driver's seat. "Anyone you know drive a white four-door sedan?"

Kimberly shook her head.

It was probably nothing. Mitch decided to err on

the side of caution when he pulled out of his parking spot and then took off in the opposite direction that he'd intended. He glanced at his rearview mirror in time to see the sedan hesitate. Was the driver watching?

He'd know in a minute.

"Where am I taking you?" he asked.

"You're coming with me, right?" Kimberly balked.

"There's no reason for us to be together. The way I see it, if someone's after you the babies are in danger as long as you're around." Saying those words were knife jabs, but he choked his own feelings back. There was no reason to give in to nostalgia. "If the people who are after you are criminals—and it sounds like they are—you'd be better off turning yourself into a government office. The US Marshals Service comes to mind. In case you haven't heard, there's a thing called witness protection."

"I didn't see anything to report," she pushed back. "I'm not a witness."

"You'd do better with law enforcement investigating your father," he stated. She didn't seem too keen on that idea based on the sharp breath she blew out.

"If all you plan to do is drop me off somewhere, you shouldn't care what I do next," she said.

"Your actions so far have put me and the twins in danger." He didn't want to admit this, but if she was determined not to bring in law enforcement, he had no choice but to watch her. He told himself that it had nothing to do with his instincts to protect his family. He could hide out for a couple of days without putting too much strain on the ranch. The image of the butchered heifer crowded his thoughts. If he put a great security team in place, he could figure out what the hell was going on with Kimberly.

His feelings toward his wife should be dead by now.

So why did the prospect of being with her 24/7 stir up feelings he couldn't afford to allow?

Chapter Six

Mitch had been driving for an hour, heading toward New Mexico. He knew of an off-grid place near the Texas border. Keeping the twins far away from Jacobstown was his priority until he sorted this out.

Kimberly settled into the passenger seat. It would take him a minute to get used to her bleached-blond hair, but as much as he didn't want to admit it, she was still as beautiful as the day he'd met her. Anger swirled like a storm cloud forming. How could he have been so off base about a person? Pride kicked him in the gut another time.

The small highway he'd been on for the past fifteen minutes turned to farm road. Since he hadn't seen a car in the past twenty minutes, he figured it was safe to stop off for a minute to make a call.

Kimberly's slow, steady breathing as she leaned her head against the headrest said she'd drifted off. She seemed to have been fighting sleep for as long as she could before it had finally claimed her.

Since Mitch couldn't be sure he'd have cell coverage much longer, he decided to pull over and make a call to Lone Star Lonnie. His foreman would be worried, since Mitch hadn't shown for their usual 5:00 a.m. roundup. No doubt Lone Star already realized that Mitch hadn't saddled up Phoenix. With the recent event involving the heifer, Mitch didn't want Lonnie worrying about him.

While most cattle ranchers used pickup trucks and four-wheelers to round up their heard, Mitch preferred horseback. A few of the men had made jokes about Mitch being a Renaissance man, but he knew they appreciated his nod to nostalgia. Heck, many of them had followed suit in the years since. The truth was that his father, who was a good man and an excellent rancher, believed in being close to the animals and never felt like he could get that sitting behind the wheel of a truck. Efficiency was one thing and no one could argue the tidiness of using a gas-powered vehicle. When Mitch had tried it out in his early twenties—probably more of a rebellion than anything else—he could make good arguments for the efficiency.

But now he couldn't imagine herding any other way. He loved his red gelding, Phoenix. The horse had sustained a supporting-limb laminitis injury at Lone Star Park that would have put most under. He'd risen from the ashes. With surgery and rehab—not to mention money and patience—Phoenix had pulled through the injury that most horses had to be put down for. It might've killed his racing career but he'd found a new lease on life on the ranch, and it seemed to suit him better anyway. The horse could cut faster and cleaner than a can opener.

Mitch kept the engine running while he stepped out of his SUV.

"Everything all right?" Lone Star Lonnie asked almost immediately.

"Fine. I'll be out of pocket for a few days and need you and the others to cover for me."

"Not a problem," Lonnie said on a relieved-sounding sigh. "We got you covered here. Anything else I can do?"

"Nah. Thought the twins could use a break with all that's been going on," Mitch said.

"Great news about Rea," Lonnie confirmed. Based on Lone Star's tone, Mitch figured his foreman understood that they also needed a break to honor the upcoming anniversary of Kimberly's death.

"We can all breathe easier," Mitch agreed.

"Any word from Zach on the heifer?" Lonnie asked.

"He couldn't get so much as a boot print from the area. Seems I made a mess of the scene and covered anyone else's possible tracks." Mitch didn't do blame, so he kept to himself that Lone Star Lonnie had trampled all over the crime scene.

Lone Star mumbled a couple of choice words. "I should've known better than to clomp my big feet—"

"I'm going to stop you right there. You had no

idea what you were walking up to or you would've been more careful," Mitch defended.

"Easy for you to say. Did you trample all over the crime scene?" Lone Star Lonnie asked with all sincerity.

Mitch drew in a sharp breath. "No. But I had a heads-up about what I was walking into. You didn't. Comparing the two scenarios is a little like asking if an apple tastes like an orange, wouldn't you say?"

Now it was Lone Star Lonnie's turn to issue a sharp breath. "No. I didn't realize. You make a good point but I'm not ready to let myself off the hook. If not for me this case might be zipped up already."

"That's one way to look at it. It's wrong but everyone's entitled to their own opinion. I know that if you'd had any idea what that could've been, you would've walked so light you couldn't have punched through a cloud. Besides, the earth is hard. There wasn't much if anything there to work with anyway by way of a footprint. It's just wishful thinking that Zach could've found anything. Not to mention the fact that there are only so many types of boots in production if the jerk who did that was even wearing them." It was all true.

Lone Star Lonnie knew it, too, because he paused before speaking. "If you didn't call about that, what's really going on?" He paused for a few seconds before adding, "I know that tone of voice, and something's wrong. Twins okay?"

The two had been friends for a long time. Lone

Star would be able to pick up on a difference in Mitch's tone.

"The two of them are fine." Mitch hesitated, hoping the right words would magically appear. "There's been a lot of stress with the doctor visit and the anniversary of…well…you know what I'm talking about—"

"I do." Lone Star Lonnie knew full well what Mitch referred to. He'd buried his wife almost a year ago. As far as Mitch was concerned, she was still dead.

"A friend of mine needed a hand and I thought it would be a good time to get away for a few days." He had no intention of committing to more than that. Being away from home for a few hours with one-year-old twins was a challenge. More than that, and Mitch would lose his mind.

"Understood. I'll take care of everything here. We'll all make sure this place runs like a well-oiled machine." Lone Star would keep his word.

"The friend I'm helping might have put the ranch in danger." Mitch wasn't sure how much he could believe of Kimberly's story so far. He also had no idea how long he could disappear with the children. Their lives had been disrupted enough without adding to it. He glanced toward the passenger's seat, wondering who in hell's name the woman occupying it really was. Damned if he hadn't been the fool who'd fallen in love with her. He remembered how timid she'd been when she first arrived in Jacobstown.

"Oh." Lonnie's tone had questions written all over it, but to his credit he didn't try to dig.

"Be careful. And keep watch at each other's back."

"Always do," Lonnie said.

"Between my friend and the heifer, I'd rather be on the ranch," Mitch said. "But I'm doing what's best for the twins right now."

"Understood. And I agree with you. If there's any danger here, the twins don't need to be around," Lonnie agreed.

With Jacobstown being a tight-knit community, Mitch couldn't risk word getting out about Kimberly. Her return from the dead would be news. Big news. And that would draw unwanted attention and visitors. No matter how many times Mitch turned it around in his head, leaving the area was the right thing to do for everyone. He remembered how quickly news had spread when Kimberly had first arrived in town. Speculation as to the mystery woman's arrival had started before her bags were unpacked. Mrs. Wilder had gone on and on about how nice it was that someone wanted to pay cash for a change instead of 3 percent of rent going to credit-card-company fees or one of those annoying new apps taking a piece of everyone's money.

Meeting Kimberly in person had taken a couple of days. Rumors were starting to spread about what she could possibly be doing at the lake house alone. Since she didn't talk to anyone and people's imaginations were often so far off base from the truth, townsfolk had decided she was either mourning a loved one or a vicious killer biding her time until she could attack. According to most that would likely happen at some point after dark or when the rest of the town slept. Hell, a few even decided she'd strike during a full moon. Imaginations had a way of getting out of control in these situations.

"Mitch." Lone Star Lonnie sounded concerned.

"Sorry." He'd dazed out with the memory, the fog of betrayal thick in his thoughts. "Be extra careful on the ranch while I'm gone and tell the others to do the same. My friend seems to think everyone in Jacobstown could be under threat—especially us."

"Because of the heifer?" Lone Star Lonnie asked, but it was more statement than question.

"Partly. She has her reasons. Reasons that I don't have the full scoop on, but until I do I'd like to operate on full alert when it comes to security. Take no chances," he warned. Mitch didn't care how unlikely the scenario was that anyone else could be targeted; he planned to warn Lone Star Lonnie and his family. "I'll be off the grid for a couple of days. I couldn't reach the others this morning. I'd like you to call a family meeting and let the others in on what's going on."

It was a big responsibility he was handing to Lone Star Lonnie, and Mitch would trust few with it. Ensuring his family was safe at all times was his number one priority.

"I'll put the word out as soon as we hang up," Lone Star Lonnie promised.

"You know how much I appreciate it," Mitch said.

"Just doing my job as your foreman and friend," Lone Star replied in a heartfelt manner. "Be safe out there."

"You know I will."

Lone Star most likely assumed that Mitch was overreacting due to the upcoming anniversary of Kimberly's death. Mitch despised lies. Even more now that Kimberly had returned and he found out he'd been living one. He'd never get his mind around how she could fake her death and walk away from him and their children.

Mitch ended the call with Lone Star and navigated onto the road.

Nearly two hours later he pulled up to a small log-style hunting cabin.

Kimberly jolted up as soon as the engine died. She grabbed her chest and glanced around with wild eyes. Fear radiated off her.

"You're safe." Mitch didn't want to be her comfort after she'd caused him so much pain. Call it ingrained cowboy code, but he couldn't stop himself from trying to help another human in need. Plus her reaction caught him off guard.

"Sorry," she said in that raspy sleepy voice that had been so damn sexy before. "I forgot where I was for a minute."

He turned and really looked at her. Too many

questions flooded his mind and he didn't want to talk when the babies were so close. The twins would need to eat as soon as they woke. Mitch also couldn't trust his temper. If she said something he didn't want to hear, he might just give her a piece of his mind. Reacting in anger was something he would've done before the kids had come along. Fatherhood had given him a new perspective.

Examining her now, he couldn't help but notice the stress cracks on her forehead and the worry deepening her dark eyes.

"Where are we?" she asked, pulling her phone out of her pocket. He didn't even think about the fact that she brought nothing with her. No purse. No backpack. Just a phone and probably cash.

Since the twins had been born, traveling light was a joke. Mitch felt like he packed up the entire house every time he walked out the front door.

"This place belongs to a buddy of mine. And you can put that thing away," he nodded toward her cell. "You won't get any reception out here."

KIMBERLY'S CHEST SQUEEZED with panic. She glanced around, trying to get her bearings. Carrying the phone she'd bought six months ago had been a tether to a world she no longer felt part of. There were no contacts in the cell, which only served to remind her just how alone she was now. She felt like she stood out without one and she figured there might come a time when she would need to call 9-1-1. "What time is it?"

"Just after seven o'clock in the morning," he supplied.

She decided to remedy at least one issue. "Put my number in your phone." She rattled off her number while he added her as a contact.

"How long was I asleep?" She rubbed blurry eyes. It wasn't like her to sleep so soundly or for this long. She hadn't done more than nap an hour or two, as best as she could, since leaving Jacobstown eleven months ago. The gravity of the current situation punched her in the gut. She'd put the three people she loved more than anything else in danger.

But how could she *not* see her family one more time? How could she *not* see how much her children had grown? Or if her husband would be showing up to the doctor appointment with another woman. The thought was a knife stab straight to the heart.

She glanced at his ring finger and noticed that he still wore his wedding band. Again her heart squeezed. She wore hers on a necklace, where it would always be close to her heart. He'd had their initials engraved on the gold band he'd given her on the day they'd exchanged vows. The band was the most important part because it stood for infinity— exactly the amount of time he said he would love her.

Looking into his cold eyes hurt.

Her mouth started to form the words *I'm sorry.* Before she could manage to speak, he pushed open the driver's-side door and stepped out. He leaned on the open door. "I'll make sure the place is clear before I come back for the twins. They'll wake if you try to pick them up, so sit tight until I get back."

And then the door closed softly and she plunged into that cold, dark feeling that had nearly consumed her before. Tears welled in her eyes but she refused to cry or feel sorry for herself.

Life was about choices.

She'd made the only ones she could in order to save Mitch and her children. She refused to think of either as a mistake. In fact they were the three biggest miracles she would most likely ever know, following the foster parents who'd taken her in and treated her as their own. Maybe her luck had run out. Maybe a person got only so much of it before it went up in smoke. Maybe it was too much to wish anything could last. Kimberly had learned early on that life took every wrong turn possible.

Twisting around to look at her babies, the sound of the door opening rocked her. Mitch could be stealthy.

"There's a hot shower if you need one. Turn on only the light you need." Mitch's deep timbre wrapped around her like a warm blanket, sending sensual shivers to places she knew better than to allow.

"You don't need me to help with them?" she asked. Maybe it was naive to think he would ask her to help with the babies.

"No." He didn't say that she'd done enough but the ice in his tone spoke volumes.

She exited the vehicle, walked inside and headed straight to the shower.

Ten minutes into the warm water sluicing over her, a knock sounded.

She panicked a little bit, realizing that she was naked and Mitch was only a few feet away. Feeling exposed, she grabbed the towel hanging over the shower rod. She peeked her head around the curtain only to find that the door was still closed and he couldn't see her.

"Did you want something?" she said for lack of something better.

"Do you want a cup of coffee?" he asked.

"Sure. I'll be out in a minute. I'm almost done," she said.

The door opened a crack. "I have clean clothes. I'll just put them on the sink and be out of your way."

"Mitch."

She waited for an answer.

"Yeah."

"Thank you for everything you're doing." She hoped it would be enough to express her gratitude. This was hard.

Mitch grunted something and then closed the door. Kimberly had no idea what he'd said and figured she probably didn't want to know.

By some miracle the kids were still asleep when she strolled into the living room/kitchen area of the cabin. The main areas were open, with a kitchenette next to the back door. There was one bedroom with a bathroom connected. The decor was simple. There was a couch and a three-piece, small, round wood dinette set. The bedroom consisted of a bed, a nightstand and a wardrobe. The place might not be much, but it felt like shelter against a raging storm.

"Coffee's on the counter," Mitch said. He stared at her for a minute before shaking his head and refocusing on the wood table, in front of which he was seated. The place had a rustic charm and looked like no one had been there in weeks. Months?

Kimberly walked over and gripped the plain white mug. It was simple and felt warm in her hands as she rolled it around in her palms.

"The best place to figure out what's going on is to start with your father. What can you tell me about him?" Mitch motioned toward the chair opposite him at the table.

She took a sip before joining him, sitting directly across from him.

"Randy Bristol was a good man. Whatever he got involved in couldn't have been on purpose or his fault, no matter how it looked," she said defensively.

"I'm not here to crucify anyone. I just want to know the truth so we can figure out the source of the threat. We both need to get this behind us so we can move on with our lives," he said.

Those last words hurt more than she could admit. She wished she could tell him what all this was about. Hell, she wished she knew.

Chapter Seven

"With you and the babies safe, I'll take off at first light," Kimberly said, hoping he would accept that on the surface, but knowing deep down that the chances were slim.

"What would that accomplish exactly?" His steel-eyed stare was as blunt as his words.

"All I needed to know is that you guys were out of danger," she said with an apologetic shrug. "You said it clearly—I'm the problem."

"So, what just happened?" He issued a grunt. "*That* was your entire plan?"

She searched the room, wishing for answers, hoping they were written on a wall, while feeling the intense heat of his glare. "Um, I don't have one. I think that's pretty obvious."

"I figured that out the minute you showed up, looking desperate," he commented before taking another sip of coffee.

"I reacted to putting you and the babies in danger. None of this was supposed to happen." Her voice climbed along with her frustration levels.

Mitch didn't immediately answer. His gaze dropped to her hands and she realized she was tightly gripping the coffee mug. She also noticed that he checked her wedding finger for a band. She forced her hand to relax by willpower and flexed the fingers of her free hand a few times. There wasn't much she could do about not wearing her ring on her finger anymore. She couldn't chance it.

He twisted his around on his finger. She couldn't blame him if he regretted still wearing it no matter how much those thoughts burned a hole in her chest.

"Consider me your shadow until we put this whole situation to rest," he continued after a thoughtful pause. His stare felt like a dare to argue.

"What would that accomplish? And what changed your mind?" She balked. He seemed determined to get away from her hours ago. "You made your point clear that you want nothing to do with me."

Before she could continue her argument, he threw his hands up in the surrender position.

"Hear me out," he started and his tone had softened a notch. Nothing in her wanted to listen. His earlier comments still stung. "Until this is over for you, it sounds like it could come back on me and the kids."

She bit her lip to keep from interrupting him, because what he was saying was true. She wanted to argue, to fight his point, but dammit she couldn't.

The reminder that *she* was putting her family in harm's way felt like pinchers latched onto her heart.

"There's no way I'll sleep at night knowing there could be a random threat out there that could pop up at any time for the twins. You already know that I work the ranch and can't be around the kids 24/7 to protect them. Plus I won't put Joyce is harm's way by leaving them with her even if I could tell her what's up, which I doubt you'll agree to."

Frustration nipped at Kimberly as she sat there, practically biting her tongue. She trusted Joyce with her kids, but all of their lives was a different story. Joyce was the most well-meaning person on the planet, but one slip and it could all be over.

"I can't argue your points." Even though she wanted to. It was unthinkable that she had caused so much pain to the person she cared most about. To that end, she wanted everyone to be safe and this whole nightmare to end. Two and a half years. Thirty long months on the run, never feeling settled or like she belonged. Meeting Mitch had changed that last part, but she'd always known it was only a matter of time until she'd have to leave him. Even then a dark cloud had hovered over their happiness. "What do you suggest?"

"We can't stay on the run with the babies, so I need to figure out where they can go that won't put anyone else at risk while keeping them safe." Mitch's low timbre washed over her, sending an inappropriate shiver racing up her arms, toward her heart.

"When you put it like that, it sounds impossible," she said in a low voice before taking another sip of coffee. Coffee might not save the world but at least it helped her think clearly. The thought of leaving her babies again nearly hollowed out her chest.

"I'd like to figure out a solution that doesn't disrupt their lives more than necessary," he continued.

"Would Joyce be able to go somewhere with them? Put them under lock and key?" she asked.

"My great-grandmother was from Gunner's Pass, a small town in Colorado. I could have Joyce and the twins brought there under tight security. I still have relatives in the area, so no one would ask questions if they showed up out of the blue," he said.

"Do you know how hard it is to stay completely off the grid nowadays? You'd have to make sure no one—and I mean *no one*—posts a picture of them online," she stated, feeling heat crawl up her neck at the thought of being separated from her babies once again. Heat that came with knowing that Mitch was on the right track and hating the idea at the same time. "Is that even possible in this day and age?" Her voice was rising, even though she tried to keep her temper and her panic levels in check. She especially didn't want to wake the babies sleeping in the next room. Although, a part of her wanted them awake and in her arms. She wanted nothing more than to hold them, feed them, *be* with them. Be their mother. None of that was realistic and she knew better than to wish for the impossible.

"We need to investigate what really happened to

your father and why. We can't do that with the babies around. *I* can't protect them *and you* and track down the truth," Mitch stated, his voice a study in calm confidence. His ability to stay cool in every conceivable situation had always been sexy to her, and it was even more so now.

Kimberly picked up her mug and gripped it with both hands. She thought long and hard about what Mitch was saying. She flipped over the options several times but there were very few. Counterarguments felt like a balloon deflating.

"You're right," she said after a long pause. "I can't disagree with what you're saying. The twins are in more danger when they're with me."

"With us," he corrected.

The feeling of hope that enveloped her with the word *us* was false at best. Mitch was a good man and that's the only reason he included himself. He was trying to make her feel better but she knew the truth. She was toxic to the people she loved, and they'd be safer without her.

"I like the idea of keeping the twins with Joyce for consistency as long as the three of them leave town and she has no idea I'm in the picture." He wasn't asking her permission, but she was grateful to be able to offer her opinion anyway. Chalk it up to cowboy code but Mitch was too much of a gentleman to cut her off. She could also see that he was an amazing father. "I'm also thinking that you're right about getting them out of Texas and keeping them out." It hurt to say that because Texas had been her sanctuary and she believed it was her children's, too. "No one will look for them in Colorado. And especially since they must realize that I'd never go back to New Mexico or anywhere near it. I'd be recognized in my hometown immediately."

"Sounds like we're in agreement," he said. "Colorado will work at least for a temporary residence. I'm planning to send top-notch security with them. It's almost the holidays and tourists will be coming and going in the town of Gunner's Pass, for skiing and the Christmas festivities. No one will suspect anything if the kids show up with their nanny, and no one will be able to trace them back to you. We'll figure out a couple of security personnel who can pose as husband and wife and fit the bill as their parents."

The thought of her children being "parented" by another couple sat like a lead fireball in her stomach. Thoughts of Mitch remarrying and giving the children another mother had shocked her out of many a night's sleep. Again, she had no right to own any of those feelings. It was her fault Mitch and the kids were in danger. So she swallowed her pride and nodded. "That's solid."

Before she could say anything else, his stare centered on her eyes.

"Are both of your parents really dead?" he asked.

"To me? Yes," she stated. He deserved to know the truth.

"Do you know where they are now?" He twisted

his wedding ring around his finger again before picking up his black coffee and taking a sip.

She shrugged in answer, and when he shot her a frustrated look she added, "New Mexico, I guess."

They sat in silence as he took another sip.

"If this is going to work, you have to be up front with me." He took off his wedding ring and set it on the table.

She stared at it like it was a bomb about to detonate. Pain could cause that kind of explosion in her chest at any second at the gesture. "I am. The people who brought me into this world walked away from me and never looked back. The people I call my parents were my last foster family."

"What about sisters or brothers?" he probed.

It was so difficult to talk about her past. "I had a sister when I was young. Lost track of her within a couple years of going into the system. I have no idea if there are others. I barely remember her."

She swiped away a surprising tear, refusing to look at him.

"Her name was Rose," she continued, not sure why she felt the need to keep talking. It had been so long since she'd been honest with anyone, with herself. "My real name is Lily Grable."

If Mitch was shocked by the admission, he didn't show it. And then it dawned on her that he would most likely suspect she'd given him a fake name. She'd had supporting documents to cover her tracks, too. Fake ID. Fake name. Fake life. With him, it had felt a little too real and a little too much like a fairy tale come true.

Betrayal scored stress lines across his forehead, resembling slash marks.

THE MORE MITCH knew about Kimb—correction, *Lily*—the better he'd be able to track down the person or persons targeting her. He was trying to get his arms around this new reality but at least this conversation was real. His life with her had been a sham, and that angered him beyond belief.

He stared at the gold band on the wooden table.

In order to help her, he had to distance himself from the pain of realizing he'd been a first-class idiot. He could look at this solely as helping someone who was lost. And the woman sitting across the table from him was the most lost person he'd ever met. Even her eyes had a lost quality to them.

It had attracted him to her in the beginning and he should've known that would come back to haunt him.

Now he wanted to punch himself for not seeing any of this coming. There'd been signs. Kimber— Lily had been the most private person he'd ever met. She'd been alone in the lake house and had seemed to want to keep it that way. Part of him could admit that he'd forced his way into her life. She'd been clear about wanting to be alone and he'd seen that as a challenge—a challenge she'd given him the green light to accept. A challenge he didn't need to rush because he saw that she wanted to be together as much

as he did. He'd planned on giving her time and space
to realize it, too. But then for reasons he still couldn't
explain, he'd shown up at her cabin that rainy afternoon. She'd invited him to come inside her cabin and
her life. The two had been inseparable after.

But still, there'd been signs.

A beautiful mystery woman staying alone in a
lake house had been too much temptation. When
she'd pushed him away—weak as her attempts might
have been—he'd seen that as a challenge, too. He
wouldn't have forced himself on anyone. A good
man wasn't built that way and especially not a Kent.
She'd given him enough go-ahead signs for him to
realize she was into him.

And when she warned him that he'd regret it if he
didn't walk away before things got too complicated,
he'd realized he was already in too deep. Mitch didn't
do "serious" with anyone. He took life seriously and
his responsibilities at the ranch. Losing his father had
intensified Mitch's serious side. Or so he'd been told
by his siblings.

He had a lot of responsibilities and he didn't take
the family business lightly.

Since rehashing the past was about as productive as chasing a ghost pepper with a shot of tequila,
Mitch picked up his ring and pocketed it. He looked
her square in the eye, ignoring the way his pulse
raced every time. "Running away from a problem
never made it better."

"All I know is there are two creeps who've been

following me around the country," she admitted. "I've been shot at and nearly run off the road more times than I can count."

It took a minute for the shock of those words to wear off. He really thought about what she was saying. Two men against her. Don't get him wrong— she was feisty as all get out. But she was no match for men with guns. She also happened to be deathly afraid of them. She was smart and that's most likely why she was still alive. What was he missing? He remembered the pair from yesterday morning. Yes, they'd been watching her. Following her. He'd suspected they were up to no good. But he didn't see a weapon. Although, it was a crowded plaza. "These men—how far away from you have they been when they shot at you?"

"What do you mean…?" She paused and it looked like she was searching her memory. "Well, I guess they've mostly shot from a distance. No. Wait. They've been close range. There was this one time in Atlanta…" She froze like she'd just given away the combination to her vault. "I guess I've been lucky every time."

He didn't like the fact that she'd closed up. He liked the fact that she didn't wear her wedding ring even less, but he was being sentimental. The marriage had been a fraud, a hiding place. Again, frustration galled him at being played like an idiot. He gave himself a mental slap. This wasn't the time to dwell on his mistakes. "Does that seem odd to you?"

A delicate brow arched. "What do you mean?"

"Seems like they'd have to be awfully bad shots to miss you so much," he continued.

"I always assumed they wanted me dead," she admitted. Confusion drew her brows together. She wasn't following.

"There's a difference between shooting at someone and shooting to kill them. I'm guessing the men who were after your foster father would be decent shots. Even a bad shot wouldn't miss every time. Probability kicks in at some point, saying they'd hit by accident if nothing else. Seems like the creeps following you knew what they were doing, considering they've found you every time. How many times have they shot at you?"

She sat there, completely still, with her gaze unfocused like she was searching inside herself for the answer.

And then light filled her eyes. "Dozens. And you're right. They sure have missed a lot."

The corner of her mouth quirked and he could tell she had an idea, a bad one at that. "Don't even think about it, Kimb—Lily."

"How do you know what's going on in my mind?" she countered.

"There's a certain twinkle you get in your eyes when an idea sparks. It's like the first firefly of summer's in there and it lights your face. And then your mouth does that thing." He pointed to the corner of her lips. "In between a pout and a smirk. When it's a bad idea that smirk is more of a frown."

Without rationalizing his actions, he reached forward and tucked a piece of her hair behind her ear.

Damn. Damn. Damn.

Mitch pulled back as if he'd touched a hot stove and mumbled a curse word. No way was he going there again.

"Lily, you're not sacrificing yourself by turning yourself over to those creeps to keep me and the babies out of danger," he ground out.

"I'm not Lily anymore. Call me Kimberly. And if they're not trying to kill me, they must want me for something. I can find out what that is and maybe stop this whole—"

He waved her off. "I said *no.*"

She issued a grunt. "You're not my boss and you don't get to tell me what to do, Mitch."

"No, but I'm still your husband and that should give me some right to talk you out of nonsense."

Now she really did shoot him a loaded look.

Damn, he wasn't trying to offend her.

"All I'm saying is that it's too dangerous and spouses have a right to warn each other." He intentionally softened his tone, unsure why he'd played the still-married card. They weren't.

She gave him another look—one that said she'd made up her mind.

Rather than debate his actions, he stood and took a step toward her. She popped to her feet in the small kitchenette and backed up until her slender hip was against the counter. He noticed that she'd lost too much weight, even though he didn't want to pay attention to those things about her. Things that made him have sympathy for her.

Sympathy or not, he couldn't let her continue down the trail of putting herself more at risk. "And then what? You go in and actually get yourself killed? Have you lost your mind?"

"Am I crazy or stupid? Say what you mean, Mitch," she said through clenched teeth.

"You really want me to speak my mind?" Heat ricocheted between them with their bodies this close. Sex had never been a problem. Neither had talking. Or at least that's what he'd believed.

He touched her arm, trying not to notice the sensual shiver that raced through him when he made contact with her.

She steadied herself for what she must've figured would be an angry spew of words.

Instead of blasting her, he leaned toward her until they were so close that he could see her pupils. But he didn't care about that. For some messed up reason he needed to inhale her flowery scent and remember that she was very much alive.

Hell, half of the time along this weird psychedelic journey, he expected to wake up next to an empty bottle of tequila. He'd welcome a hangover to the mixed-up emotions coursing through him at present. But he'd never been big on alcohol.

This close, he breathed in her unique scent— lilies and fresh-from-the-shower clean. That was her. That was Kimberly. And she was right there in front of him, after eleven long months of his chest feeling like it might cave in every time he took a breath.

Weakness had him wanting to grab hold of her and not let go.

Chapter Eight

Kimberly's hands came up to Mitch's chest, palms flat against him, and he half expected her to use them to push him away. Or hell, yell at him. To scream that he was crossing the line.

Instead she leaned her forehead against his as he dipped his head and she ran her index finger along the muscles in his chest, like she was drawing an outline that she could memorize for the next time they were separated from each other. She had to know as well as he did that this reunion wasn't going to last long, *couldn't* last long.

But this moment enveloped them both and neither seemed to have the will to fight it.

He brought his finger to her lips and traced each one. They were pink and full. Memories of how they tasted assaulted him.

Mitch didn't debate his next actions, either. He dipped his head and pressed his lips against hers.

When her lips parted and she bit his bottom lip, the air around them charged. Her body hummed with electricity as he teased her with the tip of his tongue before thrusting it inside her mouth. He dropped his hand to the nape of her neck and wrapped lean fingers around it, leaving his thumb to rest at the base. She mewled pleasure and that was all the coaxing he needed to deepen the kiss.

Her hands came up around his neck, her fingers tunneled in his hair.

Need was a lightning strike, hitting with such force that Mitch forgot where he was for a second—on the run with a near stranger. That sobering thought was the equivalent of a bucket of ice water being poured over his head.

A little voice in the back of his mind reminded him that kissing his wife was the most natural thing in the world, next to holding their children.

And that's pretty much where he knew he had to stop. Willpower was difficult to come by but he summoned up enough to pull back first.

Kimberly's beautiful eyes glittered with need, and that didn't help one bit with his self-control.

"This is a bad idea," he managed to say under his breath. His hands didn't seem to get the message because they were pulling her toward him until she was flush with his chest.

"You're right about that," she said, a little breathless. He could tell that she was trying to pluck up the courage to walk away.

It didn't help that the tiny freckle above her upper lip twinkled at him. He wanted to take it in his mouth, to taste her again. There'd been too many sleepless nights in the last eleven months in which his arms had ached to hold his wife. If someone had asked him if a body could have muscle memory for a mate and act on its own accord in mourning, he would've said hell no. That was before Kimberly. Before the wife that he loved with everything inside him had come into his life and then died.

Died.

Another sobering word. Because this close it was a little too easy to forget that the only reason she came back into his life was to save him and their children. It had nothing to do with the love he believed they'd shared.

Damn if he wasn't going soft in the brain.

Time to put the past behind and cowboy up.

"I need to check on the twins," he said, attempting to put a little space—and reality!—between him and his wife.

"Can I help?" she asked.

"I've got this covered." Shutting her down was as much for her protection as it was for his. Once this was over and she got her life back, he fully expected her to be in their children's lives. Hell, he was even happy for the twins. They'd have a mother. Having grown up with a mother who loved her children was part of the reason he counted his childhood as lucky.

The twins having to grow up without a mother was one in a long list of reasons he missed his wife.

A thought struck. Kimberly might've been his

wife but what had he really known about her? Precious little, he decided as he slipped inside the dark room with the babies.

It would be easy to let the woman step back into the role of mother. But mothering wasn't like a winter coat that someone put on when it got cold outside. Being a parent was a full-time job. The best one in the world, granted, but it wasn't for the weakhearted. He'd need to figure out what this new life would look like for all of them and maybe do a little investigating into her background before he trusted her alone with the kiddos.

He could work on finding a job in town for Kimberly if she wanted to stick around Jacobstown. Fort Worth was nearby. There was a lot of work there for anyone willing and able-bodied.

Mitch stepped lightly to the carriers with the twins inside. They slept so peacefully. He'd marveled at that eleven months ago. They didn't seem to be aware of everything they'd lost when Kimberly had died.

Babies had no sense of reality. For them, he'd seen that as a good thing. But they also had no idea how much their lives were going to change now that their mother was back.

The words seemed strange in his head.

How many times had he wished for this? For his wife to come back to life?

Would he also have to tell the twins how she'd willingly disappeared from their lives?

The babies were still sleeping, so he stepped into the doorway.

"I need to get cell coverage in order to call home. Get some rest. We'll leave when it's time to put the twins down for a nap later," he said to the woman he barely knew. His heart wanted to argue that she was still the same person, but that was a lie—everything about her was a deception.

She twisted her hands and he could tell that she was nervous. She also bit her bottom lip, which meant she was about to ask a question.

"I know that I don't deserve it but is there any chance you'd allow me to feed one of the twins?" He could see that she was holding her breath, waiting for his answer. The way she cocked her head to the side also told him that she didn't expect him to agree.

Here were the facts.

Like it or not, Kimberly was their mother.

Like it or not, Kimberly was back.

Like it or not, Kimberly was going to be in all of their lives.

The twins stirred in the room behind him. Rea belted out a cry. Time to get to work, changing and then feeding the babies.

Mitch turned on his heel.

"You can take Aaron. I'll take Rea," he said in a low growl.

KIMBERLY NEVER THOUGHT she'd have the chance to see her babies again, let alone hold one in her arms.

Joyful tcars sprang to her eyes as she held her son. He was big and strong, much more so than she'd expected him to be. Her arms ached to hold Rea, too, but she wouldn't push her luck. Holding her son was already a gift beyond anything she'd imagined in the past eleven months.

For the first time in a long time, Kimberly felt like she was home again. She knew full well that it would be a mistake to get too comfortable. There was always something or someone a few steps behind, lurking, waiting to take away everything she cared about. Anger shot through her.

This should *not* be her life.

Self-pity was a bottomless pool she had no intention of diving into.

After tearing her gaze away from her son, she locked on to Mitch's eyes from across the table. She could see the myriad of questions burning through his mind. They would have to wait a little while longer, because she had no plans to ruin this perfect moment of feeding her baby.

It was all the little things she'd missed in the last year, even the middle-of-the-night feedings and walking around, feeling half dead for most of the day. Giving her children their baths. The sweet smell of their soft, clean skin. The way they seemed to concentrate really hard to make their eyes focus enough to see her. Had they been memorizing her, too? Had they known she was temporary?

Kimberly had poured all of the love she could into

those children for that first month of their existence, wishing that it could last a lifetime. She hadn't even expected to still be alive, so holding her babies was a gift beyond measure.

Mitch's words wound back through her thoughts. Were the men trying to kidnap her rather than kill her?

If so, they must either think she saw something, knew something. Wouldn't they want to get rid of her in either case?

Unless…

It dawned on her. They thought she knew *where* something was. It's the only reason she could think of that would make them want to keep her alive. They must need her.

But what are they looking for?

She drew a frustrating blank.

Trying too hard to recall something never worked, so she focused on the angelic face of her son instead.

Those gorgeous gray eyes, so much like his father's, studied her. Did he realize that she was his mother? Did he care at this age? She'd missed so much of his life already.

Sadly, he wouldn't know any different, since she'd disappeared so early in his life. Kimberly thought about her own biological family and the mother who'd walked out on her, the anger she'd always felt toward both of her parents.

Or at least *used* to feel.

Now that she was older and had more experience,

life was becoming less black-and-white. Part of her felt sympathy for her parents. Granted, the situations were totally different, but losing children had to be the worst feeling for any parent. Even for ones like hers, who'd given them up so willingly.

Of course, life was also teaching her that there were always two sides to every story.

And an inkling of guilt said that she'd given up her children willingly, as well. She wanted to argue against the thought. But could she?

How different was she really?

Her thoughts drifted to her sister, Rose. What did she look like all grown-up? Where was she? Did she still have the lucky charm that Kimberly had fastened to a string and tucked inside her sister's pocket before the pair had been separated for good. Rose had been so young that Kimberly wondered if she even remembered having an older sibling. Kimberly had fought to keep the two of them together. Wonder Sisters—they'd given themselves the name at ages six and eight. No matter how hard Kimberly tried, she couldn't recall the details of her sister's face clearly anymore.

Lily was dead. She was Kimberly now.

That part of her, like so much of her life, had disappeared.

The past didn't have to determine her future, did it?

It was time to get her life back. Because after being with her babies and the man she—once? still?—loved, she was more determined than ever to put this whole situation with the creeps to rest. The only mother and father she'd known were gone. Her biological parents had never been in her life and never would be. Things would be different without her foster dad.

Could she find Rose someday?

The thought made her heart nearly burst. She was afraid to want it. But she had two beautiful children to reclaim. For the first time she allowed herself to consider the notion that coming back might've been something besides a disaster.

Kimberly marveled at her son in her arms while he finished the bottle.

"Bottle's empty. I've got it from here." Mitch set up a blanket with some toys in the middle of the floor before taking Aaron from her. "You should get some rest while you can."

"I'll be okay." She bit back a yawn. Considering they were planning to drop the babies off later, she wanted to spend every minute she could with them.

Mitch stared at her for a long moment after he positioned their son on the blanket. He must've picked up on her stress.

"When this all settles down, you'll get time to spend with them," he said. She shouldn't allow his deep timbre to affect her. It did anyway. Being here with their children had her heart wishing they could be something more. Like a real family.

"How do we do that?" she asked, feeling like a distant aunt when it came to knowing her own children's schedule instead of the mother she should be. She *should* know the little things about her kids. She *should* be the one to put them to bed. She *should* be the one to say when it was time for them to eat.

"I don't know." He issued a sharp sigh. "But these two deserve a mother and we'll figure it out. Right now we can't focus on anything but finding the truth of what's going on. But you have my word that we will."

Kimberly didn't want to push her luck, so she acknowledged his offering with a genuine smile. The look he returned, a brief moment of tenderness, nearly stole her breath. Not wanting to look a gift horse in the mouth, she disappeared into the other room. Sleep would be impossible. But she could rest. She could do that much for the tentative partnership Mitch had offered.

Dozens of scenarios ran through Kimberly's mind as she stretched out on the bed. Was it even possible that she could build a life near Jacobstown and be with her children? Soon, they would have to be separated again. Mitch was probably setting up the hand-off to his security team now. As much as her heart ached at the thought of being away from her babies, knowing she wasn't alone in finding answers filled her with something that felt a lot like hope.

A renewed sense of purpose filled her, too.

That feeling carried her off to sleep.

When he popped into the room hours later and informed her the babies were awake, fed and ready to go, she freshened up and quietly gathered her things before following him out to the SUV. Mitch had a baby carrier in each hand, so she opened the door for him without speaking—without needing to—enjoying the feeling of cooperation. Could they build on the sentiment?

The first real spark of hope for a future lit inside her chest as she climbed into the passenger's seat.

The twins made cooing noises in the back that warmed her heart.

"Where are we going?"

"To a truck stop off the highway to meet up with Isaac. He's been with us for ten years and I'd trust him with my life." Mitch navigated down the gravel path toward the road. "Tell me about Randy Bristol."

"My foster father owned a small rental-truck-and-van company," she informed him. "He rented mostly to businesses."

"The possibilities from that really get my brain going," he said.

"What could someone gain from using his trucks?" she asked.

"Don't you mean what couldn't they do?"

"My first thought is drugs," she stated.

"That's one possibility," he admitted. "I read in the news recently that laundering money was becoming an even bigger problem in the US. It would be easy to move with rental trucks."

"I don't know about criminal activity, though." She shrugged. "Wouldn't that also leave a paper trail? I mean people have to give a copy of their driver's license in order to rent one of my father's vehicles. If the truck ended up in a bust, the person who rented it would be easy to track down."

"The men following you could believe you have access to those files. When did your foster mother pass away?" he asked reverently. He could understand the pain of losing a mother, even though Kimberly had lived with Randy and Julie Bristol for only six years before graduating from high school. After that Kimberly had landed a full-time job and started community college. She'd moved into her own apartment near campus to be close to her favorite fosters and the only couple she considered to be family.

"The day before her birthday, three and a half years ago," she said, hearing how low her voice had become.

"I'm sorry." Mitch bowed his head so slightly that she almost missed it, and she could tell that he meant those words. He would know the feeling of losing a mother. Even though Julie wasn't technically Kimberly's mother, she loved her the same.

"Losing a mother is hard." Again his voice held so much reverence.

Did that mean a little piece of him actually still cared about her feelings? About her? Or was it just his nature to be kind to someone in pain?

"What happened to the business after your father's murder?" he asked.

"I'd planned to step in for him but everything

fell apart back home after the creeps showed up in the middle of the night," she admitted. "The office caught on fire. I was basically accused of destroying his life. His entire legacy went up in smoke, and since it was suspicious circumstances, insurance refused to release a check."

"What stopped you from going to the law then?" He quirked a brow. With his cousin being in law enforcement, essentially *being* the law, she could easily see why that would be his first question.

"Whoever was behind all of this did," she admitted. "I spoke to a deputy immediately following my father's death. I thought I was a witness. But the deputy looked at me, *spoke* to me, like I'd done something wrong and it was only a matter of time before he figured out how I'd pulled it all off."

"But did the investigation go anywhere?" He would already know the answer.

"No. The creeps showed up in the middle of the night and I took off," she stated.

"What did you tell the deputy in the interview?" he continued.

"I told them my father didn't like the water, didn't swim. I said it was odd that someone who was afraid of the water would rent a boat. But they had a distant relative who I'd never heard of mention that he said something about learning to fish." She blew out a frustrated breath. "I couldn't seem to get it through the deputy's thick head that even if that was true, fishing wasn't the same thing as renting a boat. My father did want to take up fishing. Said it would be relaxing to sit on a dock and cast out a line. But there was no way he'd do that in a boat. He'd be terrified and there'd be no use being out there."

"So he dismissed your concerns," he said.

"I asked for an autopsy. Coroner ruled his death an accident," she admitted.

"But then his business went up in flames and no one thinks to reopen the case?" he asked.

"Honestly, by then I was scared. My father's behavior had been off. He'd warned me and when I tried to figure out what was going on, ask a few questions, I was told to leave it alone and that he could handle it," she said.

"Did you tell the police about the cell phone he gave you?" he asked.

She shook her head. "He wasn't listening to me, so I kept a few things to myself. At that point I can't deny that I suspected my father of being involved in something illegal, and I wanted to protect his reputation. Fire Marshal said his office was claimed by an accidental fire set by hikers. Dry climate and s'mores aren't really a good mix according to them," she said.

"Did they track down the hikers?" he asked.

"Never found out who set the campfire because the evidence went up in flames and no one claimed responsibility," she said.

"Any chance your father kept some information off-site?" he asked.

"Yes, I thought the same thing but there was no

way I was going back to his house after everything that happened," she admitted.

"What about your place? What are the chances that something was left there?"

"I didn't keep any of my father's work files at my apartment," she said.

"Maybe he hid something when he was visiting?" He was looking for a needle in a haystack and drawing straws at this point.

"It's possible but that's a problem." She glanced at the sleeping babies in the back seat. They slept so peacefully.

"Why's that?"

"I didn't go back to my apartment, so I have no idea where my stuff is," she said.

"You didn't keep up rent payments?"

"I wasn't trying to skip out on purpose, if that's what you mean," she countered and she could hear the defensiveness in her own voice.

He issued a sharp sigh.

"I wasn't calling you irresponsible." He grunted.

"Then why don't you just come out and say what you mean?" Frustration had her baiting him into an argument.

"Fine. I will. You let your apartment go with your belongings because you were scared if you went back someone would find you. You were mourning the loss of the only person close to you and you ran away from it all instead of sticking it out and actually working out your problems. Does that sound about right?" His heated words were knife jabs to her chest.

"Guess that sums it up as you would see it," she said defensively.

He scoffed. "I'm pretty sure the world would see it like that, too."

"Say what you mean, Mitch."

The jabs were scoring direct hits and she didn't want to hear more.

"Fine. You want the truth?"

"Go ahead," she baited.

"You need to learn that you can't outrun your problems."

Kimberly shot him an angry glare. "Neither can you."

"Spit it out." Mitch was never one to mince words.

"It doesn't matter." Kimberly folded her arms. "Nothing else matters until we figure out what happened."

And that breakthrough felt about as possible as snow in July.

Chapter Nine

The balance of the ride to the meet-up spot with Mitch's security guard was spent in silence. Kimberly sat facing the door. She sniffed back the hot tears that had threatened.

She didn't know how long they'd been driving when the turn-signal clicks broke through her sour mood.

Mitch parked and got out of the vehicle before she could apologize. She needed to stay on his good side to gain his cooperation. But something inside her called out the lie. She wanted to get along with Mitch. They'd never argued when they were together before. A little voice reminded her that she'd known their relationship would be short-lived, that she would have to leave. So every minute had been precious to her and she wasn't going to spend them fighting.

Amy's face went ghostly white when her gaze landed on Kimberly. "I know Isaac told me you were okay but, damn. Seeing you here...alive..." Her gaze bounced from Kimberly to Mitch. "What's really going on here?"

"It's a long story but I'm okay," Kimberly said.

"We're supposed to be meeting with Isaac. What are you doing here?" Mitch asked his cousin. His voice left no room for doubt that he was upset.

Amy threw her hands out, offering a wide hug to her cousin. "What kind of greeting is that?"

Her gaze didn't leave Kimberly as shock turned to wonder.

"What's going on?" Amy asked.

"You can't dodge my question," Mitch insisted as Amy wrapped Kimberly in a tight hug.

"I'm sorry I deceived everyone. There were… circumstances beyond my control," Kimberly said to Amy.

Mitch grunted.

She regretted the conversation that put him in this mood. He was taking out his frustration on Amy and that wasn't exactly fair.

Amy recovered her normal, easy smile and threw a soft punch at his arm, looking put out at having to explain herself. "Okay. Fine. I needed a break from school before finals, so I came home yesterday. There. Happy now? Think he'll ask to see my Christmas shopping list now?"

Kimberly couldn't help but smile. She'd always admired Amy's spunk and figured it came in handy, considering she and Amber were the only females in a family full of alpha males.

"Isaac was supposed to bring a pseudo-wife, not my little cousin." Mitch cocked an angry brow but Amy dismissed him like he was being silly.

She turned to Kimberly and said, "Hope you don't mind that Isaac updated me."

Kimberly's chest squeezed with panic as her gaze zeroed in on Mitch. She'd been under the impression that the family knew very little about what was really going on.

"I had to brief Isaac. He has access to networks that we don't," Mitch said in his own defense.

"And your family could end up tangled in this mess." It was bad enough that she'd dragged Mitch and the babies into her drama.

Mitch blew out a sharp breath and the babies stirred.

Amy stepped between him and Kimberly. "It's what he does for a living. Isaac is used to dealing with dangerous people." Amy was the youngest. Her mother and Mitch's were sisters, and the family resemblance was striking. Amy was a couple of inches shorter than Kimberly. Her body was a stick with hips and she had a horse's mane for hair. It was the same honey-wheat as most of the Kents'. Hers was just as thick and gorgeous. Her personality, much like her hair, was a little bit untamed. "He'll be discreet about digging around to see if there's a legal trail."

Amy might be the youngest and the wildest but she was also wise beyond her years.

"I know Isaac is capable of doing his job." She'd give him that. "If anything happened to him, to *any* of you, because of me—"

Amy's hands were already up, waving Kimberly off like Isaac digging around in her background was just another day at the office.

Meanwhile Kimberly's throat was closing up on her.

He was Kent security and used to dealing with pretty much everything. He was also like family and would treat the situation delicately. At least she hoped. The idea of anyone digging around in her background was enough to give her night sweats. Law enforcement had used her background against her when her father had been murdered instead of going out looking for the actual murderer. Her record had cast doubt in the community's eyes and tainted those who were closest to her. She remembered hearing that one of the neighbors had all but accused her of burning down her father's office. He'd insinuated that she could've been involved in his death. A few had even stretched it to say they wouldn't be surprised if she'd poisoned her foster mother, Julie. Those hurt just as badly.

The memories felt like knives that were tearing up her insides. There'd been so much judgment. Hate.

Would Mitch look at her with those same condemning eyes as Deputy Talisman's if he knew about her past? He'd fallen in love with the person he thought she was. Would he have loved her if he'd known the real her?

The decision to leave New Mexico had been easy once it had become clear to her that someone wanted her dead. But if Mitch was on the right track about the creeps wanting her alive, she was really confused. She didn't know what she had that anyone else would want but had every intention of finding out.

"Why is Isaac still in the car?" Mitch broke into her heavy thoughts as he eyed the vehicle. His danger radar had been on full alert since leaving the cabin, his gaze constantly sweeping the road from all angles. Kimberly wasn't complaining. An extra set of eyes meant more protection for the ones she loved most. She'd take what she could get. Isaac worked security at the Kent family ranch and was clearly trusted.

"I asked him to stay in there until I smoothed things over." Amy's elbows came up as she positioned her hands on the hips of her skinny jeans. "He wasn't thrilled about it but I thought we should talk first. He told me what was going on when I intercepted your message and demanded to know what was going on."

Her gaze bounced from Kimberly to Mitch.

"When did you and Isaac start speaking to each

again?" Mitch couldn't let it go, and his protectiveness over Amy was another reminder of how much he cared about his family.

"Well, he had to talk to me on a three-hour car ride here, didn't he?" Amy's eyes twinkled with her smile. Kimberly wanted to hear the story behind that spark but that would have to wait. Right now, she needed to convince Amy this job wasn't right for her.

As Kimberly opened her mouth to speak, a car crept out from behind the convenience store. The hair on the back of her neck bristled.

Touching Mitch's arm, ignoring the host of other less-appropriate impulses firing, she said, "We need to get out of here."

Confusion stamped his dark features. Mitch scanned the area and almost immediately locked on to the silver Toyota Camry that was backing up to shield a good view of the driver.

"Change of plans. Get behind the wheel of my SUV, Amy," Mitch said in almost a whisper. "Kimberly, you go with her."

Isaac's gaze was focused on Mitch, Kimberly noticed. And he seemed to be picking up on what was going down.

"Get on the highway and head south for a little while," Mitch instructed as he placed his keys in Amy's palm. It was the opposite direction of their ultimate destination in Gunner's Pass, Colorado, and

Kimberly could plainly see that he was sending a mixed message to whoever might be following them.

The younger woman seemed cool under pressure, and she put on a breezy smile and hugged her older cousin. Out of the side of her mouth, she said to Kimberly, "Ready when you are."

Kimberly took in a fortifying breath. Fear assaulted her but she wasn't concerned for herself. The twins. Amy. Mitch. Isaac. They were all innocent in this mess. Anger replaced fear. She would protect the people she loved no matter what. "Let's go."

Amy made a big show of hugging Mitch goodbye. She turned to Kimberly and in a loud Southern voice said, "Ready to hit the road for our girls' trip?"

"Not sure Cancun can handle the two of us," Kimberly said as loudly as she could.

Amy glanced from Kimberly to Mitch. Amy expected them to say goodbye. Right.

She leaned in for a side hug and found herself being swept into Mitch's arms. Her breath caught as she felt that solid chest of his flush with her body. A trill of awareness followed and her chest squeezed. Mitch's actions made him seem concerned about what happened to her.

"Whatever you do..." he whispered so low she had to strain to hear him. "Don't let anything happen to those children."

"I won't," she managed to say, unwilling to admit how much she'd wanted his concern to extend to her welfare. She'd thought about the kiss they'd shared—one that couldn't happen again!—a little too much. Under normal circumstances, she might let herself dwell on any one of those things but this wasn't the time for rogue thoughts about Mitch.

He was concerned about their children. He was an amazing father. He didn't deserve any of what was happening. And neither did those two angels.

Breaking apart made her instantly aware of what her life had been like the past eleven months in the shadows. It was dark and cold. If she saw an opportunity to end this misery, she wouldn't hesitate even if it meant sacrificing herself. She told herself that she could handle anything the men did to her. But her children? Mitch? The others? She couldn't go there.

Kimberly turned toward the convenience store. How hard would it be to dart over there and give the men what they really wanted…*her*?

As if reading her mind, Mitch took her hand in his and tugged. He locked gazes. "Don't do anything crazy. The children need their mother."

The statement scored a direct hit. If anything happened to her, what would her children think? Would they know that she'd sacrificed everything to keep them safe? To make sure they lived? Or would they resent her for abandoning them?

Just like her own mother had abandoned her.

Damn. The last thought pierced her chest.

Mitch was right, so she shot him a look of acknowledgment.

Walking toward the SUV, Kimberly noticed Amy's hand trembling just a little bit as she fisted the keys.

"You watch my family and I'll keep eyes on the sedan." Mitch slipped into the passenger seat of Isaac's black hardtop Jeep. The vehicle would be agile enough to go off the road if needed, and the engine had been doctored so it would go as fast as necessary. Given that the suspect vehicle was a silver Toyota Camry, Mitch didn't expect to need to use the souped-up engine.

"Will do, boss," Isaac responded.

The Oklahoma plates also made him think the vehicle had been stolen. But then again Oklahoma plates weren't exactly unusual in Texas. The Camry topped the list of most-stolen vehicles in the US. Apparently, Mitch had read, they were easy to steal and easy to bust up in order to sell the parts. The black market for this vehicle was vast.

Mitch fished his cell out of his pocket as the sedan eased forward and then stopped as soon as the driver would be able to get a good view of the Jeep.

Discreetly, Mitch zoomed in and snapped a picture of the license plate. He immediately texted the image to Zach. He tried to zoom in on the driver's face but the picture was too grainy to make out any features. Besides, both the driver and passenger wore hoodies and reflective sunglasses.

Zach's response came within seconds.

Checking on this ASAP.

"The SUV is turning out of the parking lot," Isaac said.

As for Isaac and Amy, Mitch suspected that the silent treatment Amy had been giving Isaac had something to do with the two of them being in a relationship. If the two were dating, they kept it on the sly. And he'd been seen spending time with someone else.

For as long as Mitch could remember, she'd acted different whenever Isaac was anywhere within earshot. Her voice raised a couple of octaves and her fingers twirled in her hair. He'd come out and asked her about it once and she'd denied having a crush on Isaac, who was eight years her senior.

"No action with the sedan," Mitch informed. "Hold on. Check that. The Camry is on the move."

Adrenaline thumped through Mitch, giving him a sudden burst of extra energy. Protective instincts kicked in and he flew out the opened door.

He jumped in front of the sedan, with his cell in hand, and snapped a pic of the pair of men inside. With the Texas sun high in the sky, the sun glinted off the windshield, making it impossible to see who was inside.

The sedan swerved in time to miss Mitch and that's when he saw the end of a small barrel sticking out of the cracked window.

He dove toward the Jeep at the same time he heard the crack of a bullet split the air.

Unsure if he'd been hit, he darted into the passenger seat before another shot could be fired.

"Go," he demanded as the sedan peeled out of the lot, hot on the trail of the SUV.

Mitch glanced left in time to see blood pulsing from Isaac's neck. He muttered a curse as guilt punched him in the gut.

"You're hit," he said to Isaac.

"I'll be fine." Isaac was already unbuckled and trading seats with Mitch. "Don't let that bastard get anywhere near the SUV."

His gun was drawn as Mitch squealed out of the parking spot, racing toward the bumper of the SUV.

Mitch put on the seat belt using one hand. "Get some pressure on that wound."

Now it was Isaac's turn to bite out a few choice words. He fumbled as he opened the glove box and pulled out a first-aid kit with one hand, while trying to keep his Glock trained on the back of the Camry with his other hand.

The Jeep bounced on the potholed service road.

"Talk to me. Tell me how you're doin'," Mitch said, unable to take his eyes off the road when he really wanted to check on his employee and friend.

The Camry pushed the pace to seventy miles an hour. His stress levels weren't helped by the fact that Isaac wasn't talking. There were vehicles dotting the highway, traveling at a leisurely Saturday-afternoon pace. The speed limit was fifty-five on this stretch of road. Lower than that on the service road.

The Camry zipped around a Honda. Mitch followed, and the driver flashed high beams at him.

Yeah, I know, buddy. I'm not happy about this, either.

"Give me an update or I'll be forced to pull over," Mitch said.

"Spider bite would hurt more than this," Isaac finally said through a half grunt. It sounded like his words were coming through clenched teeth. Mitch detected the stress his friend was covering up even though he tried to come off like it was no big deal. Shock and adrenaline would keep the pain at bay temporarily.

Mitch risked a glance at Isaac. He exhaled when he saw the bleeding had been stemmed with a large quantity of gauze that was now soaked with blood. "Get out your phone and call 9-1-1."

"We've got this covered," Isaac protested.

"You're shot, bleeding and probably in shock." Mitch knew exactly what that was like. He'd been shot by illegal hunters for the first time when he was barely old enough to shave. Youth had him thinking he could push through in order to track down the responsible party. He'd overestimated his own abilities and miscalculated the men he'd tracked. Taking his injury too lightly had nearly gotten him killed.

As soon as he'd gotten close to the shooter's encampment, he'd fallen facedown from blood loss. They'd left him to die but not before getting a few kicks in. He'd come to in the hospital after his brother Will had found him.

The entire Kent and McWilliams brood had refused to give up searching until they'd found him. That was the kind of loyalty he was used to. Exactly the reason he trusted very few people besides his kin. Blood could be counted on. And after Kimberly had carved a hole in his chest, he was more resigned than ever to keep his circle closed.

"Talk to me, Isaac."

"I'm good as new, boss."

The sedan swerved in between a truck and a compact car. Kimberly and his children were a short stretch ahead and the sedan was closing in.

"I'm serious about that 9-1-1 call. Bring in the locals on this one," Mitch said with a quick glance at Isaac. Based on the amount of blood loss, Isaac wasn't in as good a shape as he claimed.

The other side of the Jeep was quiet.

"That an order?" Isaac finally asked, resignation deepening his voice.

"It's a suggestion," Mitch conceded. Was he feeling a sense of responsibility to keep Isaac safe?

Alive? Hell, yes. Isaac was the only one who could determine whether or not he needed immediate medical attention.

"I'm hit. There's blood. Another day at the office for me, boss." Isaac wouldn't give up easily. It was his job to keep the Kent family safe. He also wasn't stupid, so Mitch would take another tact.

"We gotta play this right. A lot's at stake. And one or more of these cars probably made the call already based on the way this joker's driving. We call it in and we end up on the right side of the law on this."

"Or we end up detained as suspects or witnesses while this guy gets to the people who matter most to us."

Chapter Ten

Isaac made a good point about local law enforcement. Mitch didn't know anyone out here and was outside his cousin's jurisdiction. Isaac also seemed to realize his slip—he'd admitted to having feelings for Amy. Since this wasn't the time to dig deeper into the subject, Mitch filed the information away for later.

"My phone's going crazy in my pocket. Zach might have something on the plate," Mitch said.

"That's a better person to talk to if you ask me but it's your call." Isaac's reasoning was sound. Mitch would trust his judgment.

"Zach can alert locals," Mitch agreed, not daring to take his eyes off the sedan gaining on his SUV. "Put Zach on speaker when he answers."

Isaac did.

"The Camry was stolen," Zach started right in. "A family is stranded at a gas station about a half hour from where you are now."

"I figured as much. It would've been too easy to ID these jerks otherwise," Mitch said, cutting the wheel left to avoid a collision with a blue Buick. He cursed under his breath. It was wishful thinking on his part that the driver could be identified and this whole nightmare could be wrapped up in a bow before it got messy. Kimberly had secrets that put his children at risk.

Isaac already had his weapon out, ready to shoot out a tire and slow the Camry down, but there was too much traffic and he couldn't risk a stray bullet hitting innocent people.

"Where are you now?" Zach asked.

"The last sign I read was Smithtown," Mitch informed him.

Zach cursed. "That's Sheriff Bogart's jurisdiction."

"Sounds like bad news." Mitch had to veer right to snake through thickening traffic.

"Tell me everything that's going on, starting with the vehicle you're driving," Zach instructed. "I'll need to give him a complete picture."

"You need to know something, cousin," Mitch warned. "Amy's involved."

"What's my sister doing with you?" Zach had always been protective of family, but especially when it came to his little sister.

"She came with Isaac—"

"Why would she do that? What are you guys doing in Bogart's jurisdiction, where I can't help you?" Zach's voice was steady and that meant one thing: he was working hard to control his emotions.

"I had a visitor last night. I was heading out of town with the twins," Mitch admitted.

"Devin mentioned you were helping out a friend. What's that all about?" Zach asked, still with that steady investigator's tone.

"It's Kimberly," Mitch said.

"What about her?" Zach sounded confused.

"She came back last night to warn me." Mitch paused a moment to let that sink in.

"Kimberly? As in your dead wife Kimberly?" Zach normally had more tact but he was clearly reeling from the admission.

The Camry passenger took a wild shot at them.

Mitch jammed the wheel right and muttered a curse.

"Anyone hit?" Zach finally asked after a few tense seconds.

"No, sir," Isaac reported.

"I'm fine," Mitch added. He didn't like the way the Camry zipped in between cars.

Zach issued a sharp sigh. "What else do I need to know?"

Isaac relayed additional details, leaving out a crucial fact.

"What Isaac didn't tell you is that he took a bullet," Mitch added when his security detail was finished.

"I'm sending an ambulance," Zach immediately fired back.

"Not necessary," Isaac said, trying to dismiss it.

"How is he really?" Zach asked, like Isaac wasn't sitting in the passenger's seat.

Isaac grunted his dissatisfaction.

"Took a hit to the neck. Seems to have stemmed the bleeding for now but I'd feel a helluva lot better if he would agree to have it looked at," Mitch informed him.

"A piece of a bullet scraped me, mind you," Isaac interjected. "And it's not that big of a deal."

"How's Tough Guy's coloring?" Zach asked, concern quieting his voice.

"Have no idea. My eyes have been glued to the road and have to stay there," Mitch admitted.

"The only real concern we have right now is what's in front of us," Isaac said.

"Bring 'em back on Highway 30. I'll have deputies waiting at the edge of my jurisdiction and an ambulance—no arguments, Isaac," Zach said.

"We get them back safely and you won't hear a peep from me," Isaac said.

"In the meantime," Zach continued, "I'll see how much cooperation I can get from local law enforcement. The sheriff there has a reputation for being uncooperative. Get out of his county as fast as you can."

"Once we turn around we've got a good hour and a half to go before we get to Jacobstown," Mitch admitted.

"Wish you'd clued me in sooner," Zach stated.

"We're in the same boat on that one," Mitch admitted. "This has all been coming at me at a hundred miles an hour. All I know is that Kimb—*Lily Grable* is her real name, by the way. Lily has a foster father who got himself into some kind of trouble and it was big enough to create a trail leading to her. She said she has no idea what's going on and I believe her." Mitch wasn't sure why he added the last part. It seemed important for Zach to know that Mitch trusted her. At least about that.

"Kimberly's real name is Lily Grable?" Zach asked.

"She had fake papers for the wedding that were apparently good enough to fool the man who married us. You know anything about her?" Mitch asked.

"It shouldn't take much to dig around into her background," Zach stated.

"She may have gotten into some trouble in her early teens. She was bounced around in the system," Mitch warned.

"Any juvenile records will be sealed. I'm sorry to ask this question…" Zach paused, and Mitch picked up on his cousin's hesitation.

"Go ahead." Mitch figured he knew what his cousin would ask.

"Has she kept her record clean as an adult?"

Mitch should know the answer to that. His traitorous heart said he did and that she wasn't some kind of con artist. But he'd trusted his emotions once already and that had left him with a shattered heart. "I believe so but then I thought I knew her. All I know for sure is that she's in trouble. She thinks it has something to do with her foster father's business but..."

"Get her here," Zach advised. "We can sort out the rest once she's in protective custody."

Now it was Mitch's turn to go silent. He wanted to know the truth but he didn't want to get her in trouble. Again, his heart said she wouldn't lie to him unless she felt like she had no way out.

"I'll do my best," Mitch promised.

"Until we know what we're dealing with, be careful," Zach warned.

"Always," Mitch confirmed. His children had lost their mother once. He had no intention of allowing that or anything like it to happen again. They'd been too young to understand what was going on and that had been the only grace. *Grace?* Mitch almost laughed. Nothing in his present situation fell under that category.

With the Camry taking a more aggressive stance, he had no choice but to respond in kind.

The late Saturday-afternoon traffic was thinning as they moved away from another town, but Mitch didn't like the fact that anyone else was on the road with the aggressive way he was driving. No one deserved to get caught in the middle.

The Camry started racing toward his SUV on an open stretch of highway, moving at the pace of a bullet train. He needed to cut off the Camry before it reached Kimberly, Amy and the kids.

Mitch cut the wheel left and stomped the gas pedal.

"Get Kimberly on the phone," he instructed Isaac.

THE CAMRY CAME rushing toward the back bumper of the SUV. The plates were visible in the side-view mirror. Kimberly searched for the Jeep but couldn't see any signs of it.

Amy's phone buzzed. "Can you see who that is?"

Panicked, she checked the screen. "It's Isaac."

"You should answer," Amy said.

Kimberly put the call on speaker. "Hello."

"Isaac here. How're you two doing?"

"Never better," Amy quipped and her familiarity with him brought Kimberly's stress levels down a notch. Amy's white-knuckle grip on the steering wheel belied her calmly spoken words.

"Good to hear." There was a note of relief in Isaac's voice.

Kimberly glanced at the side-view mirror again. "I lost the Jeep. Where are you guys?"

"Behind the black Dodge Ram. We're a few cars back but we got eyes on the Camry. He seems to be making a move toward you guys." He paused. "I have more bad news. We need you to turn around and we gotta get out of this county."

"Mitch?" Hearing his voice, his confirmation, would go a long way toward calming her fried nerves.

The moment of hesitation caused her heart to pound against her ribcage.

"He's right," Mitch confirmed. "There's no reason to be scared, Kimberly. I'm on the Camry and I need you headed in the opposite direction, toward Jacobstown. You hear, Amy?"

"Yes, sir," Amy confirmed.

"Don't stop or turn around. Get back to Broward County as quick as you can without being stopped. Your brother will have support waiting for you there," Mitch informed her.

Amy's grip on the steering wheel relaxed a little bit more with those words. She quirked a tiny smile and the stress cracks on the side of her eye relaxed.

"Wait a minute. You're coming, aren't you?" There was no way she was going back to Jacobstown without Mitch.

"As soon as I take care of a little problem," was all he said.

Isaac's voice came on the line. "Amy."

"Yes." Her voice perked up considerably at the sound of his. "Take the exit now."

Kimberly felt the jerk of the tires gripping the asphalt as Amy spun the wheel, cutting off a car and barely making the exit. She did, though. She swerved onto the service road and Kimberly watched as the Camry's brake lights lit up and it slowed onto the shoulder. Gravel spewed out from underneath its tires as the Jeep pulled up behind.

A shot rang out. The sound of a bullet cracking the air sent waves of panic rippling through her.

And then the SUV was fishtailing.

Amy was unfazed. She let out a resounding "Whoop!" And then she added, "Hold tight. It's about to get interesting in here."

One of the twins stirred, letting out a small, pitiful-sounding wail. The other almost immediately followed.

"Sorry, babies," Amy said, handling the wheel like a pro and straightening out the SUV.

Her driving skills were something else.

The babies wound up to a good cry in the back seat, belting out their dissatisfaction with the situation. The same feeling of helplessness that she'd felt when she'd first brought them home assaulted her.

They were older now and she was out of practice in calming them.

"What can I do?" she asked Amy, hating how small her own voice sounded.

"Binkies. Get their Binkies in their mouths. Mitch usually has them clipped to their shirts." Amy motioned toward the back seat. "Rea's should be on a Winnie the Pooh clip."

Kimberly unbuckled, climbed over the seat and positioned herself between the car seats.

"Here it is," she said after moving the strap around in order to locate the pacifier. "It's okay, sweet girl."

Kimberly hoped that her voice was what soothed her daughter enough to calm her, but it was probably just the pacifier. Her son wasn't as agreeable. It took a little coaxing, but he finally accepted the Binky and settled back to sleep.

"They're great babies," Amy said, her voice still

edged with the adrenaline shot they'd both received. "Car rides knock them out every time."

Kimberly should be the one who knew what to do instead of being wrapped in that blanket of helplessness, a feeling she hated. With the babies needing attention, she lost track of the others. "Where are Mitch and Isaac?"

Amy shrugged. "Haven't seen them since we made the turn east. Camry's out of sight, too."

Kimberly had been too caught up in trying to get the babies back to sleep to notice. Being on the road with the twins made even less sense but the thought of being away from them again was an even bigger knife to the chest.

"Mitch and Isaac will be okay and especially if they don't have to worry about us and the babies," Amy added as though she could read Kimberly's thoughts. "Isaac works security for a living. It's what he does and he's damn good at his job. My cousin has come up against some seriously bad dudes in his life. Poachers are right up there with the most dangerous scumbags, and my family knows how to handle them."

Kimberly didn't answer. Nothing was okay. Nothing would be okay again. She'd trusted her foster father. He was an honest man. Right? A little voice asked why he would've given her the phone. Why he would've warned her if that was true.

Was he involved in criminal activity? Was he a criminal? It was so hard to believe the man who'd taken her in, accepted her rough edges and had the patience to wait for them to smooth out was capable of doing anything wrong. Randy Bristol was the best kind of person. If he couldn't be trusted, no one could.

Did the mirror always have two faces? Her heart argued against the idea and her instincts backed it.

But Randy was probably the first person who'd ever been truly kind to her, and her mind constantly tried to convince her that he couldn't be a criminal.

Would she have known?

Or was she being too stubborn to see the facts right in front of her nose?

Chapter Eleven

Mitch cut the wheel right across two lanes of traffic and navigated his way onto the shoulder of the highway. The Camry was making a move toward the service road and he needed to block it before the driver traversed down the ravine. That incline was the only thing giving him a chance to catch the Camry.

As Mitch swooped around the right side of the vehicle, the passenger got off a shot. Mitch could feel the Jeep leaning heavily against its right side. It was an off-road vehicle but the roll bar reminded him Jeeps were also made for the impact that came with tipping over. Its high profile was making the tires claw to stay upright on the incline. He hoped like hell they'd dig in as the left-side nose of the Jeep pressed against the back-right bumper of the Camry.

The passenger's window went down, the end of a pistol poked out and before Mitch could react he saw that telltale flash of fire and heard the crack of a bullet.

"Windshield's bulletproof," Isaac reminded and

Mitch knew that on some level. If it wasn't he'd have been hit between the eyes based on where the windshield took impact. Even so, adrenaline shot through him like a lightning bolt.

The Camry swerved, no doubt looking for a better angle to fire off another shot.

"I'll get behind him," Mitch bit out as he stomped the brake and spun the wheel to the left, practically scraping the Camry's bumper with the maneuver.

He scanned the road. The thought of an innocent person taking a stray bullet slammed into him. At least the other drivers had enough sense to give them space. Mitch was also certain there'd be a host of 9-1-1 calls and that wasn't good since they were still in Bogart's county.

"We'll slow 'em down if I can get a good aim on a tire." Isaac voiced what Mitch was thinking.

Mitch swerved left in order to give Isaac a better vantage point. The Camry did the same.

Isaac bit out a curse as he tried to keep the gauze secure against his neck and still manage a decent aim.

"Hold on." Mitch sped up alongside the driver's side of the Camry. He couldn't get a good look inside the vehicle. There'd be no description of the driver. Just a stolen vehicle. And by now a few frantic "shots fired" calls to the sheriff's office from concerned citizens.

Isaac was right. The law would detain them and the Camry could get away, leaving Kimberly and

Amy defenseless. Amy had to watch her driving with the twins in the back seat.

The Camry banked right, making another move toward the embankment leading toward the service road. Mitch lost track of the SUV. The Camry caught gravel and swerved, creating an opening. "Now."

"This jerk is about to slow way down." Isaac took aim and fired a round.

The crack was loud inside the cab of the Jeep, causing Mitch's ears to ring. He shook it off and kept his focus on the silver sedan. There was no doubt about it—Mitch had to keep the Camry from following Kimberly, Amy and the kids.

As the sedan driver struggled to regain control from the fishtail, Mitch wedged the Jeep in between it and the service road. The incline was steep and gravel made it difficult for his tires to maintain purchase at high speeds.

Thankfully the silver sedan slowed.

As the Camry made another play for the shoulder, Mitch hesitated. The choice to keep going and risk Isaac's life or leave and risk Amy, Kimberly and the children was a hot poker inside his chest.

"Don't even think about it," Isaac ground out.

"What are you? A mind reader?" Mitch shot back even though Isaac was dead-on with his assessment.

"I know what's at stake, boss. Stay on the Camry." Then he added, "Please."

Under normal circumstances, Isaac wouldn't argue. This was extreme and Mitch was all too familiar with the guilt that came with letting someone get away who could do damage to the people he loved.

The sun was bright on the horizon, causing Mitch to squint in order to see clearly. Beams burst from the back windshield.

Mitch had cut off access to the service road, using the Jeep to block it. He prepared himself for another gunshot but instead the Camry's driver spun the wheel right into him, edging him off the road.

The tires of the Jeep struggled for purchase on the gravelly incline.

Before he could jam the brake, the Camry slammed into him, tipping the Jeep over and into a death roll.

Even with his seat belt securely fastened, Mitch's body got tossed around and his brain scrambled. Everything was happening too fast but seemed to be in slow motion at the same time—an odd feeling. One he was familiar enough with to realize his mind was playing tricks on him. It was most likely the shock coupled with another jolt of adrenaline. His brain tried to wrap around the idea that he was taking a tumble. All he could think about was Kimberly, Amy and the kids.

The Jeep sounded like it was cracking in half as it rolled.

Mitch's head snapped back before a lightning bolt of pain exploded, the aftershocks bouncing around inside his skull, creating an echo-like effect before…blackness.

Mitch heard an unfamiliar voice hovering over him. There was shouting—all male voices.

His brain cramped, his head felt like it would split in two and he couldn't open his eyes.

The smell of smoke filled his lungs. He coughed. His eyes and nose burned.

His eyes blurred as he tried to blink them open. Pain shot through him.

And then it dawned on him why.

The Jeep had rolled off the highway.

His first thought was of Isaac and then Kimberly, Amy and the children. His mind railed against the thought of anything happening to them.

And then blackness pulled him under again.

"How long do the babies usually nap?" Kimberly checked the clock on the SUV's dashboard, resigned to the fact that she'd have to rely on someone else to learn the daily habits of her children. And although she'd met the entire Kent brood, cousins and all, she'd used the pregnancy as an excuse to keep to herself. She had no idea how Amy truly felt about her and especially now that everyone knew she'd deceived them.

The younger woman had always treated Kimberly with kindness. Amy was a good person. She was most likely just being polite now for her cousin's sake. The whole Kent/McWilliams clan was tight.

Now she wished she'd gotten out more, spent more time with people. To be fair she couldn't risk having her face show up on social media pages and that was a big part of the reason she'd secluded herself. A voice in the back of her head called her out for lying.

Thankfully the Kents were a private bunch but that had lulled her into thinking she and Mitch could live a quiet life together.

She'd gone to great lengths to ensure she had legitimate-looking documentation that could prove she was Kimberly Smith. She'd given herself a new identity and believed she could have a new life to go along with it. Her judgment had been off base and her heart had overruled logic when she'd met Mitch.

She'd allowed herself to get swept up in the fantasy that life would somehow turn out all right despite the fact that the one person in the world whom she'd trusted aside from her foster mother had been involved in illegal activity right under her nose. Her stubborn mind said her father couldn't have done anything wrong. He didn't have a criminal bone in his body.

By living so much of her life on her own, she'd become good at reading people for survival. One of her foster mothers was nice after two drinks but turned into a depressed wreck after the fourth. At five, her anger turned outward toward anyone who was near. Kimberly counted drinks the first six months she lived in the Monger home. After six months she could tell how much Olivia drank with one look at her eyes. She'd become adept at identifying the tipping point where the society woman became downright mean. Thankfully the house had been large enough for Kimberly to hide in a new place every few weeks. Olivia would hunt for her on the really bad nights. The clicks of high heels against wood floors still echoed in Kimberly's thoughts.

Kimberly had learned to hide well. Olivia would eventually pass out. The next afternoon when the effects of the prior evening wore off, she'd take Kimberly out for ice cream, making sure to snap plenty of pictures to show the social worker.

That and other similar experiences had taught Kimberly to read people well. At least she believed she'd become good at it. If Randy Bristol could be a criminal, anyone could.

"They're usually awake by now," Amy said in an apologetic voice. No doubt she picked up on Kimberly's melancholy tone despite her best efforts to cover it. "Car rides always put them to sleep."

"Right. You mentioned that before and so did Mitch," Kimberly said in a low voice, making a mental note. She wanted to learn all of the ins and outs of the twins' habits. And then it occurred to her that someone was missing. Mitch had said the babysitter would accompany the twins to Colorado. "Where's Joyce?"

"She was scheduled to fly in after we arrived. Mitch didn't want anyone to know the twins were away from home. News travels fast in small towns. Joyce reported to work as usual this morning so no one would be the wiser," Amy informed her.

She shouldn't be surprised that Mitch had thought of everything.

"It's been quiet. Should we try to call Mitch again?" Kimberly turned the phone over a couple of times in her hands. All contact had been broken off and she'd been waiting impatiently for Mitch or Isaac to check in.

"As much as I want to do just that, we should wait for word," Amy said.

"You're right. I know you're right. Not knowing what's going on is hard." Kimberly could only imagine what Mitch had gone through when he'd believed her to be dead. Stabs of guilt jabbed at her stomach over the pain she'd caused.

Looking back at the babies, she couldn't help but wonder if they'd be better off without her in their lives. She seemed to bring pain and sadness to the ones she loved.

"Thank you for being so nice to me after—"

"Don't give it a thought," Amy interrupted.

"Not many people would be willing to pitch in let alone risk their life after what happened, knowing that I lied to them," Kimberly continued, wiping away a stray tear and wondering why the waterworks were springing now? She'd gone eleven months dry as a draught in a Texas summer and it seemed that the floodgates were cracking since she'd returned to the area.

Seeing her babies—and her husband—again had caused the weakness. Distance had made it easier to block everything out, to stuff her emotions down so deep she could get through the day. Feeling dead to the world was an improvement over loneliness and loss.

"I know your situation is…*complicated.* I won't pretend to understand it all. But sticking together, covering each other's backs—it's what family does." The words spoken with such conviction cracked a little more of the casing around Kimberly's heart.

Every last one of them had been part of her family. "I'm sorry for…putting everyone at risk. I was trying to protect the people I love but made a mess instead."

"We all make mistakes," Amy said with a half shrug, like putting Mitch and the children in danger ranked right up there with forgetting to pay the electric bill.

"Mitch won't forgive me," Kimberly confided. "And you shouldn't, either."

"As for me, who said I forgave you?" Amy asked with a wink. She was trying to lighten the mood. She really was wise beyond her years.

"When it comes to Mitch, he'll get over this in time," she conceded. There was so much confidence in her tone.

Could it be that easy? There was no way he could accept what she'd done, but if there was even a chance that he'd accept her as an acquaintance— could she dare hope for something more, like a partner in raising their children?—she'd be overjoyed.

She flashed a smile at Amy.

"It's nice of you to say that but he won't." Under normal circumstances, maybe Mitch could forgive family for an error in judgment. He'd view what she'd done as flat-out betrayal. And he'd be right. There was no mistaking the look in his eyes every time he looked at her now. Well, *almost* every time. There'd been something else leading up to the moment he'd kissed her.

She thought about that kiss, that moment between them that he'd shut down before feelings could spiral out of control.

They'd "been there, done that" dozens of times. A welcome-home kiss heated up until clothes were in a pile on the floor and they were tangled in the sheets. The memory caused her heart to squeeze. He was right to pull back before they slipped down that path again.

She would've stopped it herself if she hadn't been so caught up in what was happening between them, in the all-consuming, all-too-familiar heat that simmered between them until that one spark ignited an out-of-control flame.

Reality struck her again.

How much time did Kimberly have? Was there even a remote possibility that she could go to jail for her foster father's actions?

The deputy who'd interviewed her had made it clear that he couldn't wait to find evidence linking her to the investigation. If she landed in jail she wouldn't want her children to grow up knowing they had a mother who was behind bars. They would be better off believing that she was dead.

"Hey, it's all going to work out," Amy reassured.

"How do you know what I'm thinking?" Kimberly said, grateful for the attempt to make her feel better.

"You got quiet. Mitch does the same thing. Gets all inside his head with worry and stops talking to everyone," Amy stated.

"I noticed that about him, too." It felt good to remember.

She just hoped that Mitch wasn't lying in a ditch somewhere with Isaac, paying for her foster father's sins. She wasn't sure why she felt the need to confess to Amy. Maybe it was the younger woman's kindness and understanding. She had a down-to-earth quality that belied the money she'd grown up having.

"There's a mess with my father. I really don't know what he got himself into," Kimberly admitted. "He was a good man. I mean, look, he took me in when no one wanted me. I'd already been bounced around in the system. Some bad things happened to me and my younger sister before they split us up. Losing her is probably what made me lose hope in humanity."

"I'm sorry for your loss." Amy's voice held so much reverence. "That couldn't have been easy on either of you. She was all you had left. And none of that was your fault."

"It sure feels like it was," Kimberly admitted.

"You were kids," Amy said with so much sympathy, tears sprang to Kimberly's eyes.

She sniffed them back and faked a cough to cover a sob.

"Getting in trouble with the law was a choice I made, though," she said.

Amy sat quiet with a steady grip on the steering wheel.

"What did you do?"

"It was mostly petty crime, stealing. At first I did it to keep from starving but then I took what I wanted. Candy bars. I'd slip into the movies when people were coming out," Kimberly said.

Amy inclined her head and even though she never broke focus with the road, there was a lot of sympathy and acceptance radiating from her. "No wonder you wanted to keep to yourself when you first showed up."

As much as Kimberly appreciated the kind gesture, the woman wasn't hearing her. "I'm telling you that there's something broken in me that causes me to hurt people. I take what I want and leave."

It wasn't accurate to the letter but it was close enough to call.

"I hear what you're saying," Amy said after a thoughtful pause. "You might be able to convince yourself that story's true. And that's fine. But I see a strong person who has survived more than any one person should have to endure. That makes you a hero in my book, not a criminal."

Those words, that acceptance, brought out another sob in Kimberly.

"But those things I took. I didn't need them to survive," Kimberly continued, shame a tightrope around her neck, cutting off her oxygen.

"How old were you when this happened?" Amy asked.

The question threw Kimberly off guard. "Eleven, twelve. I don't exactly remember. Old enough to know better."

"When I was twelve I took a candy bar from Tom's Grocer just to see if I could get away with it. Does that make me a criminal?" Amy asked.

"Well, no. You were just being a kid," Kimberly admitted.

"Exactly. I was a good kid by most accounts. I had a good family. My brother went on to become sheriff. I knew right from wrong but I was testing the boundaries," she said. "Let me ask you this. The candy that you stole—you enjoy eating it?"

"Made me sick. I couldn't finish half of one bar," Kimberly said. "Threw the whole lot in a dumpster."

"But there was nothing wrong with the chocolate or any of the other ingredients. The bar wasn't past the expiration," she said.

Kimberly cocked a brow. She couldn't see where this was headed. "It was fresh."

"And have you eaten candy since then without getting sick?" Amy pressed.

"Of course."

"Then it would seem the action made you sick. Not the candy bar. Same thing happened to me. I couldn't enjoy what I'd stolen. I had two bites and wanted to vomit. Had to throw the rest of it away," she said. "I was too embarrassed to admit it to my family or to the owner, Tom. He goes way back with my family. He'd always been good to me. Gave me a summer job. That weighed heavy on my mind for a long time. When I got old enough to start babysitting for relatives, I learned that kids do all kinds of things while they're figuring out who they are. Stealing that candy bar taught me that I'm not a thief. As much as I can't take any of it back, I'm not sure I would if I could. I learned a valuable lesson about myself that day."

Kimberly allowed herself a small smile. She couldn't argue against Amy's logic. It made perfect sense. Her heart leaped at the thought that her actions could be forgiven so easily. She'd always been so hard on herself, she'd never once considered absolving herself of her crimes. A small part of her had believed she'd gotten what she deserved with Olivia and the others. "I guess if I'd really thought about it, I would've come to the same conclusion."

"Which proves you're not a bad person now and you weren't then, either."

Looking at the back seat, at her babies, she wasn't ready to let herself off the hook. She didn't deserve to.

And she was certain that Mitch wouldn't see it the same way. Speaking of whom, where was he and why hadn't he reached out?

Chapter Twelve

"Any word?" Kimberly asked Deputy Hanson as soon as Amy pulled the SUV alongside his in the parking lot of the Dairy Dip. They'd made it to Broward County and the sight of a law enforcement officer on their side was a welcome reprieve. Until Kimberly remembered that her real name was out there and she had no idea if she was wanted for questioning in New Mexico.

"Sheriff wants to fill you in himself," he responded. He was in his early thirties with black hair and brown eyes. He worked out and Kimberly remembered that he liked to talk about his CrossFit training. He wore reflective sunglasses and she didn't like the fact that she couldn't see his eyes.

Did Zach plan to arrest her?

"That can't be good," Kimberly said to Amy.

"They're alive, right?" Amy's voice trembled.

The deputy nodded and she blew out the breath she'd been holding.

"Follow me and I'll get us there in no time," Hanson said, shooting a look of apology before turning on his lights and siren.

The escort got them to the sheriff's office in less than half an hour. The sirens woke the babies, who cried on and off during the entire ride.

Amy shot a look toward Kimberly as though steeling her resolve. "Let's get these guys changed and fed. I can take Aaron."

Kimberly hopped out of the seat and opened the back door to her daughter, grateful to have this time with her children. The thought that she might be sent away for years sat heavily on her chest as she fumbled with the car seat buckle.

"Like this," Amy said, demonstrating the release valve.

She mimicked her and was holding her daughter within a few seconds. "Thank you."

Amy gave a quick nod. "I got the diaper bag."

Deputy Hanson was already next to Kimberly, ready to escort the women and children into the sheriff's office. Kimberly wondered if his being nice was an act. On second thought, she realized he was being especially nice to Amy. He apparently hadn't gotten the memo that she had feelings for Isaac, which also probably meant that Zach wasn't aware, either.

Once inside she half expected to be arrested.

Instead Zach greeted her with a bear hug after an equally hearty greeting with his baby sister.

Marybeth, his administrative assistant, was on her feet and circling around her desk as soon as she saw Kimberly. The middle-aged single mother had always been so kind to Kimberly. Another stab of guilt penetrated her armor.

"Good to see you, Kimberly," Marybeth said, offering a hug.

Kimberly accepted the kindness.

"Can I help with one of the babies?" Marybeth asked as her phone rang. She shot a look toward Kimberly and held her hands up. "Go on ahead. We're waiting on an important call."

Did that mean there was no word on Mitch and Isaac?

"You don't know how happy I am to see both of you," Zach said, taking Kimberly's arm and ushering her into his office.

One look at Kimberly and he seemed to realize there was no way she was handing over her baby, so he didn't ask.

Amy followed them into his office as the babies fussed.

"Go ahead and take care of the little ones," he instructed. "I'll wait."

Amy went to work, placing Aaron on the sofa and patting the spot next to him.

Kimberly took Amy's suggestion and gently placed Rea next to her brother. The little girl looked up into her mother's eyes and Kimberly felt her heart melt. Rea had the saddest little pout when she wound up to cry. She was heavier than Kimberly had expected.

Babies really did grow fast.

She quickly worked on changing Rea's diaper, hoping to hear news that Mitch and Isaac were all right.

"We can listen and take care of the kids," Kimberly urged with a pleading look.

"Mitch and Isaac are in custody," Zach informed her.

Kimberly gasped. "What did they do wrong?"

"They're safe and that's the most important part," Zach cautioned.

"Agreed." Kimberly shot a worried look toward Amy, who returned it in kind.

Joyce padded in, holding a tray with jars of baby food, along with sippy cups.

Kimberly braced for the older woman to say something mean to her—heck, give her a dirty look. Instead she set the tray down on the coffee table and then hugged her.

"I've missed you so much. It's so good to see you." Joyce used her wrist to wipe away a tear.

The emotions radiating from her children's caregiver were genuine. *She* was genuine. And Kimberly was grateful that such a loving woman had been helping out with the kids in her absence.

"Thank you for everything you've done for my family," Kimberly said to the older woman, and she meant every word.

Joyce acknowledged her with the warmest smile. "I have their favorite foods warmed. I'd be happy to help feed them while you speak to Zach. Or we can set up in the break room if you'd like privacy for grown-up talk."

If she was about to be arrested she certainly didn't want her children seeing that. But she had to believe Zach wouldn't do that in front of the children. He was a good sheriff and an even better man.

Kimberly must've given Joyce a panicked look that reflected exactly how she felt about being apart from her children even for a few minutes, because Joyce immediately proposed a different option.

"Or I could give you a hand right here," she offered.

Zach was already to his feet, calling out to Marybeth for assistance. He'd glanced at his phone more than once; the call he was expecting mustn't have come through.

Once the babies were happily being fed on the sofa, Zach motioned for Kimberly and Amy to follow him to his desk off to the right-hand side of his office.

He focused a sympathetic look on his sister. "Isaac's in the hospital. He's in surgery to remove a bullet fragment from his neck. I'm waiting for word on his prognosis."

Amy gasped. Her hand came up to her throat like she was trying to stop herself from having a panic attack.

"What happened?" A sob escaped but then she

immediately took in a breath, looking like she was reining in her emotions.

"A bullet fragment lodged in his neck, beneath his jaw. He lost enough blood to worry the EMT on the scene," he said before his gaze shifted to Kimberly. "There was an accident."

A gasp escaped before she could suppress it. Her first thought was that the children didn't deserve to lose the only parent they'd known. Mitch was an amazing father. "But he's okay, right?" She searched for any signs of mourning in Zach's eyes. Was that why he wasn't arresting her? He couldn't take both parents away from Rea and Aaron?

Nothing could happen to Mitch. She shook off the thought and refocused.

"How bad is it?"

"Physically, he'll be fine. He has a couple of bruised ribs from the seat belt, which saved both of their lives," Zach said, but there was a note of worry in his voice.

"But?"

"The local sheriff put him under arrest," he said on a sharp sigh.

Amy started pacing. "That's crazy. Why on earth would he do that?"

"It should never have happened but witnesses claimed they were shooting weapons and driving in a manner that endangered others." Zach's hands came up in the surrender position. "I'm waiting for a call back from the governor's office. He owes me a favor and I'm asking that both men be released into my custody. Of course, we'll have to wait until Isaac gets out of surgery before he can be transported nearby."

"What are the chances any of that will happen?" Amy hurled back angry words, quickly reining in her temper when her brother started to respond. "I'm sorry. I shouldn't take my frustration out on you."

"We're all fuming about this," Zach responded and there was no return anger in his voice.

He gave a reassuring look to his sister. He also seemed to realize there was more going on between Isaac and Amy than concern for a friend.

"I'm doing everything in my power to bring him home, Amy," Zach comforted. "If I have to drive there myself and pick him up, I will."

"I know," Amy said. "Between Isaac in surgery and Mitch in jail, I feel like I'm in a nightmare and can't wake up."

Welcome to Kimberly's life, she thought. Seeing the interaction between brother and sister made her think about her sister and how much she missed her.

Tracking her down now that she was old enough for the file to be unsealed would be next to impossible if Rose didn't want to be found.

But this wasn't the time to dwell on her loss. Her losses were racking up and she refused to allow anything to happen to Mitch because of her. Their children needed him. He was the stable one between the two of them. She had a past that seemed like it would always catch up to her no matter how much she tried to outpace it.

"What about me?" she plucked up enough courage to ask Zach. Bad news was like old fish—it would only smell worse with time. If she was going to be arrested, she wanted to be prepared. "You've looked into my background by now."

"I have." He gave an apologetic look.

"Whatever's in her file can't possibly represent who she is as a person," Amy defended, and Kimberly's heart swelled at the kindness.

Joyce shouted an "Amen" from where she sat on the floor, feeding the babies.

"I realize that," Zach said and his tone sounded offended.

"Glad you do," Joyce interjected. "Any one of us could vouch for her character."

The love and acceptance in the room was beyond anything Kimberly had felt with anyone else but Randy and Julie Bristol.

Grateful tears streamed from her eyes before she could get hold of her emotions. She wiped away a few tears. "You can't know how much all of this means to me."

Kimberly's ringtone sounded. She palmed her cell and immediately checked the screen.

"It's Mitch."

On instinct she spun around to face the corner and lowered her voice when she said, "Hello."

"Where are you?" There was so much concern in

Mitch's voice and she wanted it to be for her. He was most likely worried about the babies, which was fair, even though her heart decided to go rogue and wish for the impossible.

"With your cousin at Zach's office. We're all fine. But what happened to you? Zach said you were in an accident." Her words spilled out.

"The Camry knocked the Jeep off the road. We took a spill down the ravine," he said quietly. "A few concerned citizens contacted the local sheriff. Camry driver and his passenger got away. I couldn't leave Isaac on the side of the road and go after them."

"What about Isaac?" she asked. A small sigh of relief slipped out at hearing Mitch's voice and knowing he was alive. She quickly turned to a nervously waiting audience and said, "Mitch is okay."

"By the time the EMTs arrived, Isaac had lost consciousness." She could hear the heaviness in his voice.

"But Isaac's going to be all right, isn't he?" she asked.

"They separated us. He went to the hospital and I'm in lockup," he admitted. "A deputy walked in and handed me my phone. I don't know what's going on and planned to call Zach next to see if he knew."

There was noise in the background and then she heard a male voice.

"Time to go, Kent."

The line went dead.

Chapter Thirteen

"Mitch is fine," Zach said for the fourth time in the past hour. He'd done a little more digging, called in a favor and found out that Isaac was being treated at Broward County General Hospital. They had been waiting for news all night, and finally learned that Isaac was out of surgery and in stable condition, and Zach had been working on getting him transferred to nearby Dawson Memorial Hospital.

Kimberly crossed the room again, making sure to keep a calm demeanor as the babies happily played with their toys in the corner, blissfully unaware of the day's events.

She noticed that Aaron liked objects of all kinds and pretty much everything went in his mouth. Rea wasn't much different except she seemed to delight in books of all sizes and shapes.

Her daughter especially seemed to love one about animals that had fur-like substance on the dog page and other touchy-feely animals. She cooed in delight and chatted in baby talk as she patted a page.

Being with her children gave Kimberly strength and focus. She was starting to see a life with them in some way. She had no idea what that might look like just yet but she had to figure out a way to be with them again.

Life without her family made her feel like she was dead already.

Zach's desk phone rang. Marybeth's voice came over his intercom.

"It's Deputy Talisman from Hatch, New Mexico," she said.

Fear struck like stray voltage. Why would he be calling? How would he know where she was?

Zach glanced at Kimberly before walking over and picking up the phone.

After a perfunctory greeting, he said, "Would you mind repeating the name one more time?"

Kimberly prepared herself for what would come next, the same look of condemnation she'd experienced growing up. The judgment. The rejection.

She steeled herself against the pain that would come because she cared what the Kent and McWilliams families thought about her. Her gaze bounced from the door to the twins.

Amy must've been watching because she came over and sat down, taking Kimberly's hand in hers for comfort.

Zach said, "I see," a few times into the receiver.

Every time he spoke, the knot inside Kimberly's stomach tightened. Her fate was sealed and it frustrated her that everything in her life could be taken away again with the click of handcuffs.

Everything but her mind and her willpower, a little voice inside her said. Give up hope and she might as well be dead.

Zach ended the call and she took in a sharp breath.

Instead of talking, he leaned back in his chair. His gaze fixed on a spot on the opposite wall.

"What is it?" Amy asked. "What did the deputy say?"

"I'm pretty certain that I was just threatened," Zach admitted. There was a mix of surprise and anger in his voice.

"Threatened?" Amy repeated, like there was no way it could be true.

"I should probably be shocked," Kimberly said. She wasn't. "You know who I am." Although, in her mind she'd left the past behind and was Kimberly Kent, not Lily Grable. "The question is what are you going to do about it?"

"About you?" he asked. "Nothing. I told Talisman that I haven't seen you. But I have every intention of doing something about him." He turned to face Kimberly. "Tell me what happened in Hatch."

She filled him in on the way she'd been interrogated by Talisman following her foster father's murder.

"I've been in trouble with the law before." She was prepared for judgment and was surprised when she got sympathy instead. "For the record, I was a kid acting out. I'm not that person anymore. Although, there are people who would say a leopard never changes its spots."

Amy patted her hand. "It's brave of you to admit your mistakes to us."

Kimberly's heart nearly burst. She'd experienced that kind of acceptance only with the Bristols.

"You're family," Zach said. "You're one of us now. And a leopard's spots do change from adolescence to adulthood."

Those beautiful words sounded so natural coming out of his mouth. It convinced her that he believed them as much as she wanted to.

But she didn't want to put him in a bad position. "I know you can't harbor a fugitive."

"The deputy said that you skipped out of town before he could complete an investigation. All he said was that he'd like to talk to you if you showed up in town," Zach said. "He hasn't issued a warrant and was careful not to give away too much information."

"I don't understand the threat," Amy interjected.

"He said that I should be careful with this case. That it was complicated and could come back on me otherwise," he stated. "Those were his exact words."

What did that mean for Mitch and Isaac?

Before she could mount another plea for Zach to make another call to Sheriff Bogart, Mitch's athletic frame filled the doorway. She didn't think about her next actions; she just ran to him. He caught her in his arms and held her tightly against his chest.

For a long moment there were no words. Her eyes welled with tears—a surprising well had sprung in the last hour she'd spent waiting for news about Mitch.

Mitch tipped her chin up.

"It's okay. I'm here." That strong male voice of his reverberated down her neck, arms and spine.

"I was scared something had happen to you." She blinked away the tears blurring her vision and zeroed in on a large piece of gauze taped to his forehead. "What happened?"

"It's a scrape. Treated and released at the scene of the accident." His voice, his confidence, was so reassuring. She'd been a mess since this whole ordeal had begun and she wanted to wrap herself in a blanket of his confidence that everything would magically work out. It was a childish fantasy. "The Jeep rolled and I took a hit from Isaac's toolbox that got knocked loose."

Mitch shifted gears, focusing on Zach. "Any word on Isaac?"

"He's at Broward County General in stable condition," Zach informed him. "I'm working on a transfer."

Mitch kept his arms around Kimberly. He didn't seem to mind the quizzical glances from Amy and Zach. Joyce sat on the floor, playing with the children, and Zach invited Mitch to sit down.

He held tightly to Kimberly as he made his way over to the leather sofa. He made an attempt to bend down to comfort Rea but he winced with the move-ment and Kimberly realized he was downplaying his injuries.

"I can get her for you," Kimberly offered.

Mitch nodded as he eased onto the sofa. He was most likely still shaken up, and nothing more. He'd be fine once he knew Isaac was headed home.

"A deputy drove me over. I would've called to let you know we were on the way but he kept my cell until he parked out front. Marybeth signed the paper-work and then shooed him away the minute I'd been handed over. I'm technically in protective custody, pending a grand-jury investigation into the case," Mitch said as he locked gazes with Zach. "Thank you for getting me out of there."

"The charges won't stick. Sheriff Bogart should've dropped them altogether." Zack shook his head. "He's being a mule."

"That reminds me. I owe a call to Harley," Mitch said and Kimberly recognized the family attorney's name.

"He'll see to it Bogart focuses on finding the bad guys instead of wasting his time with me," Mitch continued. "A name came up. Ever hear of anyone called Baxter?"

Everyone's gaze shot to Kimberly.

"Never heard the name before." She shrugged.

"I got a partial description of the men in the Camry when I overheard a deputy talking."

Kimberly had never gotten close enough to the

men chasing her for an accurate description. Her heart hammered her ribs.

Zach perked up at the news.

The thought of putting faces to the male figures frightened her.

"One of the males has light blond hair. He was described as being short." But then Mitch would most likely already know that since he'd seen him at the medical plaza. "Maybe five feet eight inches. He's built like a male gymnast according to witness accounts. The other one is a couple of inches taller but definitely shorter than six-feet tall. He has black hair and a runner's build. Both are being considered armed and dangerous—obviously. The sheriff informed his deputy that he's about to put out a bulletin that both are wanted for fleeing the scene of an accident. Both were wearing aviator sunglasses and hoodies. Similar to when I saw them in the plaza."

"What plaza?" Zach asked.

Mitch brought his cousin up-to-date.

The descriptions weren't much more than they already knew. She stared blankly at the wall.

"You've never seen the men before they started following you?" Zach asked, striking his keyboard with decisive finger strokes.

"No," she responded. "Wish I knew who they were. My father didn't say anything about new people hanging around, either."

"Fair enough." Zach paused. "Nothing about the

descriptions strikes a familiar chord? Nor does the name Baxter?"

"No. I doubt there's any trace of this guy. He wiped out my father's business with a fire, no doubt to cover any documentation of their business transactions," she informed him.

"People use fires to cover tracks. They also use them to cover crimes," Zach stated.

"I do feel like my foster father's truck-rental business is key. I mean why burn it down otherwise in either case," Kimberly said. Without a criminal case pending there was no way for Zach to get more information. No agency cared about her foster father's death.

"I haven't gotten any bulletins in the system," Zach said.

"Do you think Bogart's involved?" she asked.

"Based on his reputation, he's not playing both sides of the law. He could be scared, though," Zach admitted.

That made two of them, she thought.

"Tell me more about your parents. What kind of people were they?" Zach questioned. He had to know it was a dead end but she appreciated the effort he was making. And he was most likely just killing time while he waited for a hit in the system.

"Mom was incredible. She volunteered at my school when I came to live with them. She'd been working full-time on Dad's business and said it was a nice change to have something else to focus on.

She said I was good company even though we both knew it was a lie when I first came to live with them. Dad was a rock. He was always lending someone his personal vehicle if they didn't have money to pay for one of his rentals. Mom used to say he had a heart of gold. She was right." It was nice to refer to him as Dad again, like she'd begun calling him junior year of high school. She'd bought him one of those super-cheesy #1 Dad coffee mugs from her part-time job selling pretzels at a kiosk in the mall. He'd teared up when he opened the present. Then he'd surprised her by asking if she'd like to call him by that name instead of Randy. She'd shocked herself by saying she would. They'd both had a good cry that Christmas morning. Her foster mother, Julie, had joined in, wrapping both of them in a warm embrace. It was then that their family seemed to click. Life seemed easier and Kimberly felt like she belonged somewhere for the first time in her life. Tears streamed down her cheeks at the memories. When she shook off the reverie and looked up, everyone in the room had become intensely interested on what was in front of them or in their lap.

She cleared her throat, swiped at a few stray tears and continued, "They put up with me and acted like my antics were no trouble."

"What kind of antics?" Zach asked but there was no judgment in his voice like she'd expected to hear.

"Flunking a history test so hard it should've been embarrassing after my mom had spent the entire night studying with me." Kimberly looked toward the window that bathed the room in sunlight. "I expected her to lose her temper with me after that. Maybe grab a switch from outside like so many others had. I knew that material inside and out." She paused. "All she did when I walked through the back door after school was hug me, hand me a bowl of chocolate ice cream and tell me I'd get the hang of taking tests."

"Sounds like an amazing woman," Mitch said with so much reverence, goose bumps raised on Kimberly's arms.

"She was. The best." Kimberly had to suppress a sob. She could admit to still getting emotional about her mother's death. Kidney disease had been a slow, painful way to go. A woman who was so...*good*... didn't deserve to die like that.

Kimberly's being there by her mother's side as she left the world was the only consolation. The two had held hands until her mother's had gone slack.

"I didn't stop there. I guess I wanted to prove by that point that I was as unlovable as I felt," she admitted.

"It's normal for teens to test the boundaries," Zach said. "With your background, I'm surprised your behavior didn't get a whole lot worse."

"It did." Admitting this next part—the part about being a criminal—hurt. But the family had been so kind to her and they deserved to know everything at this point. "I broke into a neighbor's barn with a guy I'd been sneaking out to see. He seemed so tough, like he could handle anything. He'd made a trip to juvie and I thought he could teach me how to live in the real world and show the Bristols there was no saving me. Mark coaxed me into taking a couple drinks of beer. At least, that's what I thought it was. Turns out he'd laced it with that popular date-rape drug. Thankfully the owner came home and caught him before he could follow through on..."

Kimberly looked down, trying to get a handle on her emotions.

"...his *plans*."

"How old were you when this happened?" Mitch asked. His voice was a low rumble of anger.

"Fifteen," she answered. "My fosters pleaded for leniency and the judge must've been feeling good that day because he let me off with time served after my arrest and three years of probation. He wouldn't have had to do anything, though. I was so freaked out by the whole experience when I realized that Mark could've done anything he wanted to me. I never wanted to be that vulnerable again." She glanced at Mitch. "Which is the reason I didn't want champagne on our wedding day. I can't stand alcohol."

"You could've told me before, Kimberly," he said and his voice was soft this time. "I would've understood."

She needed to change the subject or she might get lost in that same sense of comfort that had caused her to make so many mistakes in her life recently. Even with the Bristols she'd never felt the sense of home that she did when she was with Mitch. He was her true north. But letting herself get lost in that feeling again would be a mistake. Even if her current situation could be cleared up—which she highly doubted would happen with her still being alive—what would happen next? Something had always come along to mess up the scarce few good situations in her life.

She also needed to change the subject before she got wrapped up in the warm sensations that would cloud her judgment when the time came to split again.

"Why would Sheriff Bogart suspect you had anything to do with what was going on?" Kimberly asked Mitch, picking up Rea and moving to the sofa. She set the baby in between her and Mitch. The feeling of being a family overwhelmed her. It all seemed so natural. The three of them sitting on the sofa together. But it wouldn't last; it *couldn't* last.

Mitch and Zach exchanged knowing glances. What was that all about?

"Mr. Clean would be jealous of your spotless criminal record," she added.

"Not important." Mitch glanced at her so quickly, she almost didn't catch it.

And then it dawned on her why.

"It's because of me, isn't it?" she asked. "He suspects you because of my criminal background."

"It doesn't matter," he said, focusing on Rea.

Her daughter was innocent and beautiful and full of potential.

Birds of a feather, she thought. Mitch was most likely arrested because of his association with her. Her reputation would damage her innocent children's lives. They'd be better off never knowing her than to be hemmed into that same box as she'd been her whole life and *would* be for her entire existence.

"That's not fair to you. You had no idea what was going on. That's part of why I never told you anything. Exactly so you would never be put in this position." She reminded herself to calm down for Rea's and Aaron's sakes. Her past would follow her for the rest of her life, tainting everyone around her. When word got out about her faking her death and her involvement with this Baxter person—whoever he turned out to be—her children would be labeled, too. Anger churned through her. It wasn't fair. People made mistakes. Why was it so hard to shuck the past and start fresh?

"I'm sorry," she whispered.

"No need to apologize," he said quickly. "It is what it is."

That might be true. But her presence dragged down the good Kent family name—a name she wanted her children to be proud of precisely because of the one she'd been given.

The name Grable was most often associated with unemployment, get-rich-quick scams and deceit.

No matter how right it felt to be with Mitch and

their children in the moment, Kimberly's background would always be an albatross around their necks.

If she stuck around.

Chapter Fourteen

"We have to get the babies to a safe place and get out of here," Kimberly said in a whisper to Mitch. He was confused by the changes in her. When he'd first arrived she'd practically thrown herself into his arms. Now she was keeping her distance.

She was suddenly acting strange toward him, sending mixed signals. He couldn't ask her what was going on outright. She seemed too aware of everyone else in the room. Her occasional longing look toward one of the babies had him concerned. He was thankful she seemed to want to include him in the plans she was cooking up. Mitch wondered if the others in the room were picking up on her increasing anxiety.

"Or we could let the law do its job and find out who murdered your foster father," he said quietly.

"How did it feel to be interrogated like a common criminal?" she responded.

"It wasn't a trip to the State Fair but that *is* part of a law-enforcement investigation. At times innocent people have to put up with being inconvenienced while the investigator gets to the bottom of what's really going on." Based on her reaction so far, it seemed like there was more to the question than she was letting on. "Why?"

"Long story," she said a little too defensively. So there was something to his suspicion.

Since she seemed determined to shut him out, he decided to bring up the subject again later.

"Think Zach's finding anything?" she asked, her hands twisted together.

"We'll know soon enough." On closer examination she looked wiped out. Dark circles cradled her brown eyes. She looked like she'd spent the last couple of hours on the edge of her seat and her exhaustion was starting to show.

Mitch took her hand in his to reassure her, ignoring the frissons of heat the contact produced. "We'll sort this mess out and I'll be right here until the end."

Kimberly sat there, still, for a long moment. Was he getting through? She had so many layers of defense built up. So much more than when he'd first met her.

"You shouldn't make promises that you can't keep," she said after a thoughtful pause. "And now I've put everyone in danger. I shouldn't be here."

Then she stood up and crossed the room without looking back.

Zach walked over to Mitch.

"She'll come around," Zach said, taking a seat next to his cousin.

To what?

What would she be coming around to? Joint custody? Friendship? Something more? Trust was big in Mitch's book and she'd obliterated theirs.

She'd had her reasons and, he could admit, most of them had to do with him and their children. Put in her shoes, would he have done the same thing?

No, he wouldn't. But then he'd grown up with a huge support network and more people who had his back than he could count.

What had she grown up with?

Parents who weren't fit and had abandoned her before she was old enough to fend for herself. Heartache from losing the only sister she'd ever known and had tried to protect. Then there was a string of people who'd let her down in the years when she needed stability the most. There'd been others who'd taken advantage of her and used her as a workhorse, abused her. She'd been through hell and back when he'd had the love and support of five siblings, two cousins and two of the best parents a kid could hope for.

Had life been easy for the Kents?

Hell no. They suffered the same as everybody else. People they loved died just like everyone else. They experienced the world as everyone did—heartaches and happiness.

They'd been brought up to know the value of a hard day's work, that money bought food and other necessities—not necessarily happiness—and that they could always count on one another when life handed them hard times.

He examined Kimberly and wondered if she'd ever be able to break down the walls she'd constructed to protect herself.

Then again what exactly was he offering her?

"Jordan called to see if I'd heard from you," Zach said.

"I need to call home and let the rest of my brothers know I'm all right," Mitch conceded. He'd been wrapped up in trying to figure out what was going on and hadn't checked in with any of his brothers. Of course, everyone would be worried by now. He could kick himself for not thinking about his family. His heart wanted to argue that his family was right here in the room with him. And that part was true. Kimberly was the mother of his children. She would always be connected to him. Family.

Thinking of the ranch brought up the issue of the heifer.

"Have you made any progress on the investigation at the ranch?" he asked his cousin.

Zach shook his head. "My first thought was teenagers playing a cruel prank."

"They'd have to be pretty damn twisted to think that was funny."

"Or on something that distorted reality," Zach agreed.

"Jacobstown's never had a drug problem." Mitch arched a brow.

"Not prior to this, if that's what we're dealing with," Zach stated.

"But that's not what you think now?"

"Town's in an uproar. Social media has been going crazy with speculation. Everything from high teenagers passing through from Fort Worth to a cult traveling in the area," Zach admitted. "There's no shortage of speculation on who or what might've been involved. A few have pointed toward an illegal trapper."

"I'm guessing you're not refuting the claim," Mitch said.

"No. I'd rather folks go down that trail than some of the others, which have them ready to break out pitchforks and take shifts guarding Main Street," Zach said with an eye roll.

"People can get carried away," Mitch agreed.

"Thing is the only tracks leading up to the heifer belong to you and Lone Star," Zach continued.

"Seems strange that you couldn't find anything else," Mitch said.

"I did. I found marks leading away from the scene," Zach stated.

"What kind of *marks*?"

"Like a tree limb being used to brush over someone's tracks." Zach ground his back teeth. "Might be nothing. Old. There's evidence teenagers have been slipping onto your property to hike."

"Nothing new there," Mitch said, but his mind was flipping over possibilities.

"Everyone's on guard right now. At the very least they're seeing this as a bad omen," Zach informed him.

"Could've been an illegal trapper," Mitch said after a thoughtful pause. That area was his brother's responsibility. "Will checks the fences on that side of the property. Maybe he was near and spooked the guy who then covered his tracks as he bailed."

"I'll keep my eyes peeled the same," Zach mentioned.

"We'll keep on the extra security we hired just in case there's foul play," Mitch said.

"Good idea."

Zach informed Mitch of his offer to take the babies, along with Joyce, to his house.

"Is Kimberly aware?" Mitch asked. It should be strange to include someone else in the decision-making process when it came to his children. It wasn't.

"Yes. She wanted to ask your opinion about it," Zach answered.

Amy came over and sat next to Mitch.

"Kimberly okay?" she asked before correcting herself. "Never mind that question. How could anyone be sane under the circumstances?"

He nodded in agreement.

"I just spoke to Isaac," she said, and he could tell she was trying to keep her tone as even as possible. Her eyes were brighter, though. She chanced a glance toward her brother. "He's going to be released from the hospital and into my brother's custody tomorrow."

"He should probably stay at my place while he heals," Zach offered.

"Knowing Isaac, he has an opinion on the matter," Mitch said. He shot an apologetic look in Amy's direction. "He's been seen around town with Hailey Jepson. She might want to weigh in, too."

Amy needed to know, but Mitch didn't like being the one to give her the heads-up about Isaac's personal business. It was better she hear the news from family, though.

Aaron fussed, throwing the toy that had been keeping him occupied.

"I'll go help Kimberly," Amy said. She couldn't get to her feet fast enough after Mitch's revelation. Again, he hated to be the one to inform her but he didn't want her to think she had another chance with Isaac if she didn't. Mitch had it on good authority Isaac was seeing Hailey now. He had no idea how serious the relationship was. He'd been out of the loop on most issues since inheriting the ranch and losing Kimberly. But Amy deserved to know what she was up against.

One thing was certain.

Relationships were tricky as hell.

Speaking of which, Kimberly was on her way over to Mitch and Zach.

She stopped in front of Mitch.

"What do you think about the babies staying with your cousin temporarily?" she asked.

"He'll take care of them. Make sure they're safe," Mitch stated.

Zach nodded.

"Then how about you and me get out of here." She made a show of yawning. "I'm beat and I can't think straight anymore. I just had another cup of coffee and I could've been drinking water for the effect it had. I need to grab a couple hours of sleep. What about you?"

It was pretty obvious to Mitch, and most likely Zach, that she was making the move she'd been in the corner contemplating for the past hour.

"I can use a few hours of shut-eye," he admitted, curious as to where she was planning to go with this. There was a corrupt deputy in Hatch. He was pretty damn sure of that. How far up the chain did the deception go?

Mitch had a feeling they'd figure it out soon enough because Kimberly had that focused look in her eye.

"Then, let's take off."

KIMBERLY PINCHED THE bridge of her nose to stem the raging headache threatening to crack her skull in half. The plan to leave the babies in Zach's care and get away from Jacobstown was solid. The borrowed truck from his cousin Zach wasn't as comfortable as the SUV but should keep them both under the radar.

She leaned her head against the headrest and started counting exit signs. "Do you think the babies will do okay without you there? You've been the steady force in their lives."

"The whole family plans to check in with them. Joyce will be there 24/7. They'll be surrounded by people who love them," Mitch said.

"It's not the same as having you there," she countered. The idea that her babies had so many wonderful people to depend on warmed her inside and out. No matter how much she wanted to be the one who put her kids to bed every night, she realized that might not be possible. Not if Baxter got what he wanted. It was clear that he wanted something from her. What would happen if he got it? She doubted a criminal would let her live long enough to be a witness no matter how much she pleaded.

"There'll be no shortage of folks to fuss over them." His tone was certain while she was churning like a blender inside.

"Will they be able to sleep somewhere besides their own beds?" she asked, picking up her cell and then turning it over and over in her hands. She couldn't risk having photos of them on her phone in case those jerks got to her. She'd envied all the mothers she'd come across in the past eleven months with prominent pictures of their children as their wallpaper. In conversation, which she'd avoided as much as possible, she'd had to lie about having babies of her own.

Since she was on the run and her heart belonged to Mitch anyway, dating had been out of the question. *Everything* about a normal life was out of bounds in the life she'd been living.

"You saw them in the SUV. They'll do fine at Zach's," he said and there was a hint of sympathy in his voice.

Snapping them into their child seats in Zach's personal vehicle had caused her heart to beat in painful stabs. The air had thinned. She couldn't breathe. She'd blame it on the humidity thickening the air but all the threatening clouds had cleared up after a brief shower and it had been sunny ever since.

"If you say so." She had no personal experience to draw on with the twins when it came to their sleep schedules. The last time she'd put them to bed they woke every four to six hours to feed.

They'd be safe at Zach's, a little voice in the back of her head reassured. At least she could count on that much.

"Mind if we change the subject?" Mitch asked, and she appreciated his thoughtfulness.

"Go ahead."

"What do you really think happened with your dad?" he asked. "Deep down."

"Gut level?" she asked.

"Yes. What do your instincts tell you?" he pressed.

"I can't prove it, but I know he wouldn't do anything illegal or immoral. The man once drove an hour in one of his rentals to buy a refrigeration system so he could deliver food to a town that had been hit hard by layoffs, all of which came out of his pocket. If a store clerk accidentally gave him too much change or forgot to charge for an item, he'd turn around and go back. I mean, seriously, he'd turn around for fifty cents so the cashier would balance all right at the end of the night. So whatever was going on I'm thinking that he couldn't have really known about it," she informed him. "He could've been mixed up in a crime accidentally or seen something he shouldn't have. In which case no one should be looking at me."

"Unless they're thinking the same thing and figuring you might've gotten him involved in some kind of trouble," he reasoned. His point was valid.

"I might've made mistakes as a kid but it shouldn't be difficult for an investigator to figure out that my life has been clean since junior year of high school," she said a little defensively. No matter how well she'd been living her life since then it was still hard to talk about the person she'd been. Thinking back to the manner in which the investigator had grilled her made even more sense. "Disappearing most likely didn't help matters."

"We already know there hasn't been a warrant issued for your arrest. We have a name. Baxter. And Zach is knee-deep in the investigation," Mitch offered.

"Which means more people are in jeopardy because of me," she said on a sharp sigh.

"People are in jeopardy because of a criminal," Mitch interjected. "My cousin deals with bad people on a daily basis. He knows how to handle himself."

At least he knew to be careful and take the threat seriously.

Mitch shot a quick look of apology before focusing on the stretch of highway ahead. "Did he and your mother take in other foster kids?"

"None that I know of. I never asked and there weren't any pictures around," she said. "Seems like there would have been some evidence."

"Sounds like the kind of guy who'd give the shirt off his back if someone needed it," Mitch said.

"He was." She thought about the young guy who'd shown up at the back door on her last visit to her father's office. "Maybe this all had to do with someone my father was trying to help." Was it wishful thinking? Or had he crossed the line? The more she thought about the man Randy Bristol had been the less him being a criminal made sense. "There was this guy. I never really got a good look at his face or maybe I just wasn't really paying attention. He was in his late teens, maybe early twenties. Thin. He had long hair that he kept in a messy braid. Think I heard my dad call him Tonto once. Have no idea what it meant."

"Do you remember the name of your caseworker when you were in the system?" he asked.

"Absolutely. Old Train-wreck Turner. I got lucky with the Bristols. Train-wreck placed me in some nightmare homes before them. She didn't care where I ended up." She glanced at him in time to see his fist tighten around the steering wheel.

"She still live in the area where you grew up?"

"It's possible." She shrugged. "Been a long time since I've been home, and I lost contact with her the minute I turned eighteen."

"I'm guessing that was on purpose," he stated.

"Didn't see a point keeping in touch with someone I couldn't trust or stand," she admitted.

"Take my phone out of the cup holder and text her name to Zach if you don't mind," he said.

She palmed his cell and entered the password he'd supplied, noticing that he'd changed it from her birthday to the twins'.

Everything else on the home screen looked the same as the last time she'd used his phone, so it was easy to navigate.

Zach replied almost immediately to the text with a thumbs-up icon and a promise to get back to them ASAP.

"He's on it, but I doubt she'll be any help. She was pretty old and has most likely retired since then."

"Let's hope for an address by morning," Mitch said. Then he added, "Might want to tell him about Tonto."

"Okay." It was most likely nothing but it couldn't hurt. She entered everything she could recall about Tonto. "Done."

Another thumbs-up icon popped onto the screen.

Mitch took the next exit and then followed GPS on his phone to the nearest cash-based motel.

After parking on the opposite-side lot and doing a quick check-in that required no ID, she followed him into room number six. The external door leading straight to the east-facing parking lot wasn't ideal from a security standpoint but paying in cash was more important since it didn't leave a digital trail.

The room was typical for the price. Two well-used mattresses topping a pair of full-size beds were separated by a small nightstand. There was a lamp, notepad and pen, and landline telephone sitting on top. If Kimberly had to bet, there'd be a Bible in the drawer.

"Shower's in the back." Mitch pointed to the only place it could be.

Ten minutes later she came out wearing a towel. Mitch handed her a toothbrush and toothpaste, which was manna from heaven at this point.

"Do I want to ask where you got these?" She made eyes at him.

"It's okay. They're fine. Came from camping supplies in the trunk of the SUV," he said.

She must've scrubbed her teeth for five minutes.

"There's a clean T-shirt on the bed. It's mine but you're welcome to it," he practically growled as he passed her and his low rumble of a voice sent sensual skitters across her skin. She recognized that tone, and intense, hungry, passionate sex usually followed.

Suddenly aware of just how little material covered her, she gripped the knot on her towel to secure it.

An exhale of relief followed as he kept walking, because being this close to the only man she'd given her heart to was its own hell. Add the sexual chemistry that constantly pinged between them and it was draining to keep fighting what her body deemed as the most natural thing.

As she walked past him, he caught her arm. She stopped and faced him.

"Where'd you go last year?" There was so much emotion present in his eyes. A mix of hurt, anger and something else...something much more primal simmered between them. *Hunger.*

Letting the chemistry between them rule would be a huge mistake and yet her feet were planted.

"We should get some sleep." The words sounded hollow even to her.

She couldn't.

"Kimberly." That one word was spoken so loaded with emotion that her breath caught.

Heat ricocheted between them as they stood this close, barely more than a foot apart. Where his fingers touched her forearm, tingles of uncapped sexual energy pulsed.

"It's better for both of us if I don't say where I've been hiding out."

"Why? Because you plan to disappear again when it gets tough? Use those same places to hide?"

She turned her face away, not wanting to look at him. "Maybe."

"On our wedding day, did you mean those vows

or were they just empty words to you?" No emotion was present in his voice now and she couldn't read him when she glanced up.

She should lie. Tell him what he seemed to need to hear. That it was all a fake and she'd never loved him.

She couldn't.

"Yes."

"Then why didn't you trust me enough to tell me the truth?" he asked.

"Because you would've gone all cowboy code on me and tried to fix my problems," she shot back, feeling anger rise in her chest.

"Isn't that what married people do? Face down trouble together? Stick by each other's side?"

"Yes. But—"

"Never mind." There was so much finality in those words. "Get some sleep."

Kimberly wished there was some way to tell him she was sorry for the past, a way that didn't feel like an insult to his pride.

She couldn't.

So she stood on tiptoe, wrapped her arms around his neck and kissed him.

Mitch pulled back. His eyes were closed. His mental debate was written across the stress cracks on his forehead.

"I'm not trying to cause more pain," she said in a low voice. "I just missed this. I missed you so much I didn't think I could breathe. And I'm tired of fight-

ing against what my body wants when you're anywhere near me."

"We cross that line and I can't undo that," he said,
pressing his forehead to hers.

"Do you want me, Mitch?" She tugged the knot
on the towel free and let the cotton material drop to
the floor.

Standing there, naked, in front of the man her
body craved should feel awkward. She should be
embarrassed about her body like she'd always been
before Mitch. But this was Mitch. He was her husband. And though a piece of paper had declared her
dead, she was very much alive. Very much a woman.
Very much reacting to the sexy male standing in
front of her.

"That's not the right question to ask." His warm
breath sensitized her skin. He brought his hands up
to her hips, where they rested on either side of her
body. Contact sent currents of heat coursing through
her body, seeking an outlet.

"Then, what is?"

Chapter Fifteen

Mitch trailed his fingers up the sides of Kimberly's hips in a lazy *S* curve. He took in a sharp shot of air before he ran his flat palm against her belly—the place that had given him two beautiful children. She had more curves since giving birth and her skin was milky-soft perfection. *She* was perfection.

Kimberly's hands went to the snap of his jeans. His hands joined hers and a few seconds later his jeans joined her towel on the floor. He shrugged out of his T-shirt next and then she helped him take off his boxers.

"I thought I'd lost you for good," he said, hearing the huskiness in his own voice.

"I'm here, Mitch." The sound of his name rolling off her tongue was the sweetest damn sound he'd heard. Hell, he should be angry right now. He couldn't be if he tried. His feelings ran too deep. He'd missed her too much.

There she was, standing right in front of him.

Consequences be damned—he couldn't let himself care about the fallout from doing one of the most basic human needs—making love to his wife.

Mitch took a step toward her. He took her hands in his and braided their fingers.

A beat later, she pressed her body to his. Their hands broke apart but made immediate contact with skin. Her flat palm went against his chest, her fingers running along the ridges of his pecs.

One of his hands found her chin and lifted it to better angle her mouth toward his. He took his sweet time kissing her even though his body cried out with urgency. He had no plans to rush this moment. He'd waited too long, wanted it too much. There were split seconds where he thought this couldn't be real, *she* couldn't be real.

Mitch wrapped his hands around her waist and pulled her body flush with his. Skin-to-skin contact caused his erection to strain. Urgency escalated but he was a disciplined man. Or so he thought until her hands tunneled through his hair and her sweet tongue darted inside his mouth.

He needed to think about something else besides the soft feel of her creamy skin and her quickening breath that matched his own. No way was he allowing this to be over before he could really get started.

An attempt to focus on the paperwork that needed to be done at the ranch when he returned lasted two seconds. *Way to crush being in control, Mitch.*

He trailed his fingers along her soft curves until he palmed her nipples. They pebbled with contact.

He rolled them around between his thumb and forefinger and then swallowed her sounds of pleasure.

Kisses intensified. Hands searched. Pleasure mounted.

Kimberly opened her eyes, caught his stare and then said, "Make love to me, Mitch."

He picked her up and she wrapped her legs around his midsection. He carried her the couple of steps to the bed before setting her down and dropping to his knees.

Before he could locate a condom, she'd wrapped her fingers around his shaft and was guiding him inside her. "We better hold on a second."

He didn't want to stop this but had to.

After fishing an old condom out of his wallet, he returned a few seconds later and she helped roll it down his shaft. She bucked her hips—she was ready for him—until he reached deep inside her. Her eyes were wild with passion when she looked up at him. He drove himself inside her, hard and fast, as he gripped both sides of her hips, digging his fingers into her sexy round bottom. She moaned and rocked harder on his erection, driving him to the brink.

His mouth found hers and his tongue slid inside her mouth, searching for the sweet honey there.

He tightened his arms around her beautiful body and bucked deeper inside her sex. She matched him stride for stride.

Urgency built, demanding release.

Mitch slowed his pacing for a second, trying to

gain control, but it was useless with his wife in his arms, bodies melting together as her internal muscles quivered around his stiff erection.

Her breathing quickened and she bucked harder and faster until their bodies were a frenzy of electric impulses.

He detonated a few seconds after he was certain that her body was drained.

Instead of relaxing, she rode a second wave with him as his body exploded with sexual impulses.

She pulled him down on top of her as they caught their breath.

Quietly, in barely a whisper, he said into her ear, "I never stopped loving you, Kimberly."

KIMBERLY JOLTED AWAKE out of deep sleep. It took a second to get her bearings. She realized that she was in a motel room an hour from the New Mexico border.

Rolling onto her side, she felt around the bed. The room was dark. No doubt the blackout curtains were still drawn but she had no idea what time it was.

Mitch was gone.

Reaching out, her hand landed on an object. It crinkled. Paper? She reached onto the nightstand next to the bed and located her phone.

Using the flashlight app, she picked up the note. *Be right back. M*

The door burst open, causing her to jump.

Mitch hustled inside, locking the door behind

him and flipping on the light. "Time to get up. We gotta go."

"What is it?" she asked, already to her feet and gripping her phone so hard that she noticed her knuckles had gone white.

"Baxter's creeps are here."

She muttered a curse as she jumped into action, throwing on clothes and gathering what little supplies they had as she tossed them into the backpack.

"What are we going to do?" she asked.

"Get out of here alive." He ate up the space between them in a couple of strides, took the backpack from her and shouldered it.

He took her hand—and this wasn't the time to think about where they stood romantically, but it did flash across her mind—and gave a quick squeeze. Her heart practically danced from the look in his eye when he made eye contact with her. Things had changed. She didn't know what that meant yet but it was a sign things were moving in the right direction between them.

"How do you plan to do that?" she whispered.

"They found our vehicle, but not us," he stated.

"So they're on the opposite side of the parking lot?"

He nodded as he opened the door and led her outside. The sun was breaking against the horizon and during this time of year that meant it had to be around 7:00 a.m.

There was a Denny's restaurant next door to the motel and a crossroad to the highway.

"We get out of sight long enough for the area to clear and we get the vehicle back. Or we make a new plan." He nodded toward a cluster of warehouse-looking buildings across the road. "For now our best chance is to find a place to get out of sight before they figure out which room we've been in."

The sound of a window breaking crashed through the quiet morning, save for the occasional car on the highway whooshing by. They could hear the noise but could not see the road.

With the creeps closing in Kimberly was grateful the babies were safe with Zach and Amy and nowhere near the motel. A thought struck that if anything went down, both of their parents could be dead. She crouched down low—trying to squash any such possibility—as Mitch did and followed him across the road toward the row of buildings, unsure what frightened her more—the thought of dying or living without her family.

Nothing could happen to either one of them. The twins deserved to grow up with both parents.

"Mitch," Kimberly said as they cleared the road and got closer to the cluster of buildings. "I'm truly sorry for everything I've put you through. Loving you was the most selfish thing I've ever done."

"Loving someone else isn't selfish," he countered, and she was surprised at how quickly he'd responded.

"It is for me. I've done nothing but hurt you and I must've known on some level that I would," she said.

He didn't answer right away as they rounded the corner of a building and he stood upright.

Mitch spun around, looped his hands around her waist and tugged her toward him. He captured her lips with his. When he'd kissed her so thoroughly that her knees almost buckled he pulled back and said, "You tried to warn me. I didn't want to hear you. You brought me back to life, made me feel something deeper than I've ever felt before. If anyone's to blame, it's me. You told me there was no room in your life for me, and I took advantage of the fact that you wanted this as much as I did."

"You couldn't have known about...*this*." She waved her arm toward the motel.

"No. But I've never felt more alive than when I'm with you. I just don't know what that means when all this is over. I'm questioning how I could let my feelings run out of control with someone I never really knew in the first place." Mitch had grown up in Jacobstown and lived on the family ranch his whole life. She could see where falling for a stranger would throw him off. But those last words were daggers to her heart because she felt like she knew him. It was odd, really, but she felt like they'd had this deep connection from day one. The kind that made her feel like she knew him at the most intimate level even though he was right that they didn't know basic facts about each other, like family medical history. But then again she didn't know her parents' medical history, either. Mitch would know his. His parents had been the bedrock of the community. From everything she knew they had been decent, upstanding people who'd loved their children.

"We should find a place to hunker down until the coast is clear," Mitch finally said.

He managed to find an unlocked vehicle and they slipped into the cab of the pickup. He closed and locked the door behind them before opening a small box underneath the dashboard.

"What are you doing?" she asked.

"Checking to see if I can hot-wire this thing if there's no other option," he admitted. He played around with something she couldn't quite see before he repositioned himself to cover her.

It was light outside. If anyone came near the truck they'd see one or both of them. But this was the best they had to work with at the moment. There were steel doors on the warehouses with similar-looking loading docks. None would be easy to break in to.

"I'm sorry that I lied to you about my parents," she said in a low voice. "I was embarrassed to admit that I don't really know who they are. All I was ever told was that I was left in that parking lot and when no one claimed me and my sister, we were dumped into the system. I was seven years old. Now, I have no idea where they are or what they're doing. I don't even know if they're alive. I don't want to care either way but I guess I'm curious about my past. Where I come from. My caseworker tried to keep my sister and I together for as long as possible, or so she said. But when one of my foster dads knocked my little sister into the wall for chewing her food too loudly I lost it."

"That couldn't have gone well for you," he said and his voice was steady, unreadable.

"He said I was violent and they believed him over me. His wife lied to my caseworker, saying that I'd become too hard to handle but that Rose was still okay. She never cried. Not when one of them was listening. I heard her at night when the lights were turned out. She'd sniffle for hours. Sometimes I'd crawl into her bed but that was dangerous because I got in trouble if I didn't stick to my own. And some nights, I'd be so tired that I'd fall asleep. Those lead to bad days," she said. All those memories bearing down on her like heavy weights pressing against her chest made it hard to breathe.

"No child should be treated that way," he said. His voice was low but there was palpable anger in it. "Did you ever ask about your parents?"

"No. What would be the use? They didn't want me." She heard the hurt in her own voice even though she'd spent years building up walls that made it impossible to feel when she thought about her past.

"History, for one," he said. "The truth, for another."

"I know everything I need to about them. They rejected me." A few tears welled in her eyes but she refused to let them fall.

"How can you be certain?" he asked.

"Because they left me behind at a strip mall with

my sister. They took off and didn't look back. They just left me and my sister and that was it." She heard the defensiveness in her tone.

Mitch got quiet, like he did when he was angry. "I'm sorry you went through that, Kimberly. You deserved better."

She kept her voice low so he wouldn't hear.

"That's where you're wrong. *You* deserved better."

Chapter Sixteen

Mitch heard voices. The men were coming. He silently cursed for not thinking to bring his shotgun. He'd kept all of his weapons locked up since the babies had arrived for safety's sake.

"Hey, Ron," one of the men said. "They have to be here somewhere. We're not leaving without her."

"The spotter's sure it was them?" Ron responded.

"Bet his mother's life on it," the other creep said.

"Baxter's none too thrilled she's gotten away this long," Ron said.

Spotter? Rental vans and trucks. A picture was emerging that caused Mitch to grind his back teeth in anger. Those elements added up to human traffickers. Hatch, New Mexico, being situated near the Mexican border, was the perfect gateway.

Based on the picture Kimberly portrayed of her foster father, he didn't seem the type to be involved in a human-trafficking ring—a ring that could be paying the local sheriff's deputy to look the other way. Pinning their crime on an innocent woman could provide cover. Tonto might've provided transportation, and that's where Randy Bristol came in. Maybe the kid came asking for a favor, pretended to be in trouble. Then again maybe he'd gotten in over his head and Bristol was trying to dig him out.

Mitch would share his suspicions with Zach as soon as he and Kimberly were in the clear.

A truck door opened and closed. Then another. They were checking the trucks first.

"Climb over here on my side," Mitch instructed. He had to get her out of there. Hell, get them both out of there. This was a no-win situation. He searched around for a spare key.

It was wishful thinking and a waste of time.

Mitch risked a glance at the side-view mirror.

The man on his side had a pistol, so he assumed the other one did, too. The half dozen trucks in between wouldn't take long for the creeps to clear. They moved quickly, methodically checking the cab of each truck.

Mitch cranked the window down, thankful these older models didn't have automatic buttons, which would require starting the engine and, therefore, a key.

"They want me. Let them take me," Kimberly said, hoisting up her phone. "I can put on GPS and you can regroup and find me before anything happens. You said yourself that they aren't trying to kill me. It'll give you time."

"Not a chance. We have another option," he said.

"Mitch. Listen to reason. They don't need you, which means they'll shoot to kill," she continued.

She made a good point.

But there was no way Mitch would willingly allow her to give herself up to save him.

He couldn't let the men get any closer.

There had to be a better plan.

"Promise me that you'll try to get away," he said.

She didn't respond.

"Kimberly. Promise me."

Another beat of silence passed before she finally said, "I promise."

"Good. I'll create a diversion and I need you to run like hell around the side of the warehouse." He fished keys from his pocket and handed them to her. "If you make it to the truck before me, don't wait."

"Mitch—"

"There's no time to argue. I'll be fine. They want you and there's no reason to kill me," he said but he knew they'd take the shot in a heartbeat. He hoped they were bad shots. Either way he had every intention of making it home to his children. "If we get separated, get out of here and make contact as soon as you're clear."

"I will if you will," she committed.

"Deal." Now all he had to do was get them both out of there alive.

"What's the plan?" She popped her head up and checked her side. "My guy's getting close. He's two trucks back."

"No matter what I say in the next thirty seconds, stay right here and keep your head down." Mitch opened the door and hopped out before she could put up an argument. He slammed the door shut behind him, glanced at his guy and then darted toward the warehouse.

"Run, Kimberly. Get out of there. They found us. Go," he shouted as he ran. He darted around the side of the building, praying she'd stay put.

The crack of a bullet split the air.

His heart thudded.

He paused long enough to listen for footsteps. Heard them. The *clomp-clomp* of two sets of boots meant both men were on his tail.

He checked the window for an alarm system. Found one. The blinking light near the office door was a welcome relief.

He picked up a rock and slammed it against the glass of the door. The small pane shattered, bringing an ear-piercing alarm to life.

Soon police would descend on the cluster of warehouses. They'd anticipate a threat.

Mitch listened for the footsteps but couldn't pick up the sound over the shrieking alarm. The men should've rounded the corner by now.

Which meant they'd most likely doubled back to Kimberly.

He muttered a curse as he turned back and pushed his legs as fast as they could go. As he rounded the corner, he slammed into an object full force.

After he was knocked off his feet, he immediately popped back up.

He leaned against the building to regain his balance as blood dripped down his face. His brain scrambled for a split second but he forced clarity.

Diving into the knees of his attacker, he knocked the guy off balance. The guy had a runner's build. The Runner proved his strength with a jab to Mitch's gut, followed by a knee to his groin.

Mitch had control of the guy's gun hand. Being shot at point-blank range wasn't in the plan today.

The Runner bucked, knocking Mitch off balance. The next thing Mitch knew he was facedown, eating gravel. The move knocked the gun loose. It scraped against concrete as it spun out of reach.

Mitch tried to twist around but was blocked. This guy was using Mitch's considerable size against him, beating him to the punch.

That was about to change.

Mitch spun one way and then shifted to the opposite direction. He slammed his fist into the Runner's jaw as he tumbled sideways.

The move gained Mitch enough of an advantage to climb on top of his opponent. Police sirens—a welcome relief—sounded.

He scanned the parking lot for Kimberly. The distraction gave the Runner an opportunity to land a punch hard enough to snap Mitch's head back. He spit blood as he tightened his thighs to a viselike grip and pinned the Runner's right arm underneath Mitch's left knee.

Tires squealed to a stop on the cruiser. The driver's door flew open and the business end of a gun was pointed at Mitch.

"Get your hands up," the officer shouted in the authoritative voice he'd heard Zach use with suspects.

Mitch threw his hands in the air and shouted, "There's a weapon ten feet from us on the ground. This man tried to shoot me and I defended myself."

The Runner struggled.

"I want both of your hands in the air. Now!"

As soon as Mitch lightened his grip, the Runner made a move.

"He's not going to cooperate and I'm not dying out here. Tell me what you want me to do," Mitch ground out as he pinned the Runner down again.

Another cruiser blasted in beside the first.

"Freeze." The cop moved closer, weapon leading the way.

"I can't. Not until this guy stops fighting," Mitch countered. "My name is Mitch Kent. My cousin is the sheriff of Broward County."

That seemed to satisfy the officer as he moved toward the weapon on the ground. He kicked it out of the way.

The second officer, gun aimed directly at the Runner now, came up alongside Mitch. He holstered his weapon and palmed zip cuffs.

Mitch got a good angle with his thighs on the

Runner and then held his hands up. "This man shot at me and my wife. She's in a truck, waiting for me. There's another man."

When he put two and two together his heart fisted.

The second guy was nowhere to be seen.

That meant one thing.

He had Kimberly.

MITCH WAS AT the sheriff's office when he really wanted to be out searching for Kimberly. The truck had been empty, just as he'd feared. It had been half an hour since the parking-lot incident, and the Runner wasn't talking.

The only shred of hope he could hold on to was the knowledge that Baxter had wanted her alive.

Another fifteen minutes and the plane carrying Zach would land at the private airstrip ten minutes away from Sheriff Anderson's office.

Every minute lost while sitting in an office, doing nothing, was excruciating.

To be fair, the sheriff had every available man hunting for Kimberly.

The Runner had been identified as Ron Sawyer. He had a well-known association with Paul Baxter. Baxter ran one the larger human-trafficking rings in the southwest. There was an obvious connection to Randy Bristol's van-and-truck-rental business but like Kimberly had pointed out, her father's industry was heavily regulated. Even so, a man who'd give his shirt off his back would find a way to help someone in need—and that person in need was Tonto.

Mitch's cell buzzed in his pocket. He prayed that it would be Kimberly, letting him know that she was safe somewhere. It was unrealistic. The truck was still in the parking lot when he and the deputies had checked.

Zach's name popped up on the screen.

"Hello," Mitch answered.

"I have news." That Zach didn't prep him one way or the other sat heavily on Mitch's chest.

"Go ahead." He paced.

"The name Kimberly supplied came back with a hit. Tonto, otherwise known as Kenny Tonornato by his given name, is dead."

"How'd it happen?"

"He was tossed out of the back of a vehicle on a road leading to the Mescalero Reservation, which is not a far drive from Hatch," Zach informed him. "His wrists and ankles were bound..." Zach hesitated. The news was about to get worse. "There was a bullet wound in between his eyes. He was shot at point-blank range with a 9 millimeter."

Mitch muttered a string of curse words.

"He was a good kid who'd had it rough. Neighbors of the family reported that he was trying to work odd jobs in order to raise enough money to bring his grandmother across the border. She needed medical help. His mother was worrying herself sick." Zach paused.

"The pieces aren't hard to put together from there. He was getting desperate to help his mother, so he went to the person who could get the job done and bring his grandmother to the States," Mitch said. "Baxter."

"Only, that kind of help comes at a price. He tells the kid to get a truck," Zach continued.

"And the only person he knows with one big enough is Randy Bristol," Mitch said. "Who also has a heart to match."

"Which explains why a decent man would willingly lend out a truck to a known criminal," Zach stated. "Because he thought he was lending it to Tonto. When he put two and two together he thought he could find a way out, thus the warnings to Kimberly."

Kimberly needed to know that the man she knew and loved as her father wasn't a criminal. Mitch wasn't sure why that was so important to him but it was.

"I thought you should know what we found," Zach said.

"Thank you doesn't begin to cover my gratitude," Mitch stated.

"It's what family does for each other. You'd do the same if the shoe was on the other foot." Zach was dead on. "Speaking of which, those bogus charges against you and Isaac have been dropped."

"As they should have been." Mitch was never more grateful for family than he was right now. Between his brothers, sister and cousins there was always someone who had his back. He returned the favor, too. There was a sense of belonging in that.

What did Kimberly have?

There had been two people she trusted before the age of eighteen. Both were gone. One was murdered.

She'd held steadfastly to her belief in her foster father's innocence no matter how much evidence mounted against him.

If Randy Bristol was guilty it was because of his kind heart. She'd said herself that he'd give the shirt off his back to someone in need. Tonto was a young kid, barely of age, who needed a helping hand. A man like Bristol wouldn't have let him down—that was the kind of man Mitch hoped he was. He could see himself tripping over the same wire. There must have been some paper trail in the rental agreements that could lead authorities to Baxter.

He sure as hell had no intention of disappointing Kimberly.

Mitch glanced at the clock.

An hour had passed since he'd last seen her, with no word on her whereabouts.

Chapter Seventeen

Kimberly's head hurt to the tune of feeling like someone had run a pitchfork through it, stabbing her multiple times.

Pain shot through her skull as she opened her eyes. A thumping noise pounded in her ears. She could count each beat of her heart.

"Sleeping Beauty's awake." Her gaze zeroed in on the quiet voice in the corner of the small dark room.

Sweat dripped off her nose as she tried to reposition herself to get a better look. Her wrists were bound together. She angled her body and quickly realized the same was true of her ankles.

She scanned the small space for Mitch. And then for the other creep when she couldn't find her husband.

It was just the two of them.

For now.

He'd obviously just alerted someone to the fact that she was conscious. She tried to memorize her surroundings so she could lead law enforcement back when she broke away from this creep. Her eyes strained to see in the dim light.

"Who are you?" she asked. He knew she was awake so there was no point in trying to pretend otherwise. Maybe she could get some information from the creep who was built like a male gymnast. His hair was black as night. The reflective sunglasses he wore most likely covered brown eyes. He wore jeans and a collared shirt, and the underarms were stained with rings of sweat.

He sat in a fold-up chair. His frame blocked something... *What?*

She noticed the creep's hip holster, too, with a handgun in it. She had no idea what kind it was and wished she'd taken Mitch up on one of his offers to teach her to shoot a gun. She knew enough to realize that there was a safety mechanism that had to be flipped before the gun would fire. If she got close enough to him to take it, she would need to remember that.

Memorizing details about the creep caused hope to blossom that she might make it out of there alive.

Baxter wanted something from her. Is that who he'd called?

"Do you have a family?" she asked, hoping to get him to speak to her. He'd ended the call without another word and set his phone in his lap. He leaned toward her, clasped both of his hands together and rested his elbows on his knees.

The creep was chewing a mouthful of tobacco. He leaned to the left and spit.

Kimberly felt the hard concrete against her body. Each movement hurt, so she must've racked up some bruises on the way down.

Her mouth was dry, making it difficult to swallow. Dust was everywhere and the building couldn't be bigger than ten by twelve feet. A shed? The red clay on the creep's boots said she was in West Texas or New Mexico—most likely the latter.

Was she back in her hometown? A chill raced down her back.

Where was Mitch?

Panic nearly doubled her over at thinking anything could've happened to him.

The heat gripped her, making it difficult to breathe with all of the dusty clay filling her lungs when she tried to make a move.

This place reminded her of home. The dry air. The heat. If they weren't in New Mexico, they were close.

"Sit tight," the creep said. He had overly tanned skin—orange? Did he wear too much self-tanner? His face could only be described as squatty. Much like the rest of him—tree-trunk arms with a thick middle and not a lot of height. He looked strong. The man could bench-press Arnold Schwarzenegger.

The last thing she remembered was being dragged across the parking lot, with a viselike grip secured around her waist, before she was struck with something hard on top of her head. A rock? The butt of a gun? His free hand had covered her mouth so she couldn't scream for help as he toted her across the parking lot and away from Mitch.

She had the headache to prove she'd received a serious blow.

"Where's your friend?" she asked when she got no response from her other questions.

"In hell with your boyfriend," he shot back.

Kimberly's lungs almost seized but she covered her reaction with a blank face. Mitch had to be alive. The twins needed him. His family needed him. *She* needed him.

"Tell me where I am and why I'm here," she said.

He issued a grunt.

"You telling me that you have no idea?" he asked, his voice incredulous.

"Would I ask if I did?" She wished she could reel in the sarcasm as soon as the insulting words left her mouth.

Luckily he didn't seem offended. That or he didn't realize he was being insulted. Either way she wouldn't look a gift horse in the mouth. She wasn't sure if she should tip her hand and let the creep know she knew about Baxter.

She could throw out another name and see what response came.

"Is Tonto involved in this—whatever *this* is?" she asked.

"Not anymore."

Her heart pitched. From what she could tell, Tonto

wasn't out of his teens yet. He wasn't much more than a kid. And the creep's grin said all she needed to know about what had happened.

"So you killed him. For what? I don't have any money. My father wasn't a wealthy man," she said, trying to hold back tears at the senseless loss of life.

"Tonto was stupid," he said. The smug smile said he'd most likely done the dirty work himself.

"Stupid people drive past me on the highway every day. Doesn't mean they should die."

"No one refuses a job from the boss." There was disdain in his voice.

"I doubt we're talking about a legitimate business," she countered. At least she had him speaking to her. "Maybe he wasn't a criminal."

"You're right about that. He was too weak—"

"To what?" she interrupted. "Hurt innocent people?"

"No one asked him to hurt anyone." He balked. "The kid would've slept with the light on the rest of his life if he had to walk one day in my shoes."

"Then what was the job?" she prodded.

"To give you up," he said like he was reading a cereal-box label. *Twenty-six grams of sugar. Zero carbohydrates. Kill a kid.*

Her breath caught.

"What do you mean by that?" she regained composure before he could see how much hearing those words hurt. Were they true? He could be playing her. Trying to throw her off track.

"He wouldn't tell us where you'd run off to hide."
He sneered. Spit.

Everything inside her wanted to break free of her
bindings and hurt this soulless creep.

For the sake of her children, she would play it as
cool as she could.

The door swung open, causing beams of sunlight
to bathe the room. She blinked against the sudden
burst of light, trying to make out the male silhouette
moving toward her. She prayed that Mitch would
walk in behind the guy.

When the door slammed shut, she could see again
after blinking her eyes a few times.

"It's about time we finally meet." A man with
tight-cut hair that was graying at the temples strolled
in like he was walking into the lobby of the Four
Seasons Hotel.

"Baxter." It was more of a statement than a question.

"There's no need to be so formal. You can call me
Paul." He wore dress slacks and an expensive-looking
collared shirt. The material was fine—maybe silk.
He seemed too—she didn't know—clean-cut to be
a criminal. Too well dressed to get his hands dirty.
But then again he most likely had lackeys, like the
creep, for that.

Another thought struck. This one lodged a knot
in her stomach.

Would a criminal let her see his face or give out
details like his first name if he planned to let her live?

The voice of reason in the back of her head shouted a resounding *no*.

Her heart hammered her ribs at thinking about her babies. The twins…and Mitch would have to live without her if this man had his way.

If she had to die today, she wanted her children to know she'd gone out fighting…fighting for them… fighting to stay alive so they could be a family even if that meant shared custody and every other Christmas spent together. Her heart wished for more, for Mitch, for a family. But that was wishful thinking.

Now that she'd had a taste of being with them again there was no way she could go back to being on the run alone.

In being face-to-face with the man she was sure had killed her father and ruined her life, she expected to hate him, to want to lash out. And part of her did. But another side to her—the side Randy and Julie had influenced—felt something she didn't expect to feel, compassion.

Was she frustrated? Yes.

Did she feel a sense of loss? Yes.

Did she hate Paul Baxter? No.

Instead she felt pity. The man standing in front of her was a coldhearted shell. She couldn't hate him no matter how much a part of her wanted to. She saw a little piece of herself inside his cold blue eyes— eyes that the world had hardened. And she wondered if she hadn't met the Bristols would she have gone down a different path?

A man like Baxter would only ever live half a life. He'd never know the best gifts in life—true love, kindness and forgiveness. And she was beginning to see the first step to healing was to learn to forgive herself.

A man like Baxter would only know hate and revenge.

A man who lived on the rim of society, preying on innocent people, would need two eyes in the back of his head for the rest of his life because someone would always want to rise up and take him out in order to replace him.

The world he lived in was violent and brutal.

She was even more grateful for the gift of her foster parents. They'd taught her how to reach deep inside herself to become a better person. They'd forgiven her mistakes—a lesson she was still learning. They'd taught her the meaning of real love.

In doing so, they'd given her a life. They were the reason she could open up to Mitch and let love inside. Real love. And if she survived this…nightmare…she would work as hard as she needed to in order to deserve his trust again.

"Whatever it is that you think I have, you're going to be sadly disappointed," she told him. "You destroyed my father's business. I have no money. I've got nothing a man like you would want."

Baxter motioned for the creep sitting in the chair to move out of his way.

As the man stood up and shoved his chair to one

side, a metal container came into view—a safe. More than that, her father's safe. She'd forgotten about the small safe he'd had tucked away in a specially built filing cabinet in his office. He'd shown it to her the day after her eighteenth birthday. No wonder she'd forgotten it existed—that was seven years ago.

"Open it," Baxter demanded.

"I can't. I don't know how. Never seen it before in my life," she lied.

The expensive leather of his shoe caught the side of her cheek with full force as he kicked her. She let out a cry—a weakness she immediately quelled— as her head snapped back. She felt the cool trickle of blood. Her jaw felt like it was going to explode from pain.

"Are you trying to play me?" Like a shark circling its prey, Baxter walked a ring around her, each step quicker than the last. He reminded her of a prize-fighter in the ring, working up to his next punch. "You and I both know Tonto gave your father photos and statements implicating me and my men. I'm not leaving here without the evidence."

She let her body go limp on the concrete and then curled into a ball to protect her vital organs.

"You better get to work," he demanded. "Figure it out."

"I can't," she admitted, holding her breath to steel herself for the next blow.

It didn't come but she didn't dare look up or speak again. She'd read an article about grizzly bears while waiting for a bus once. It stated that if one came charging toward a human, the best possibility for survival was to curl up in a ball and play dead. That's exactly what she did, figuring it couldn't hurt.

A moment later she felt herself being jerked up to sitting position. She curled her arms around her bent knees, hugging them to her chest.

"I'm not lying. I can't help you. Why don't you just use a sledgehammer?" she said. She knew the combination at one time but that was years ago.

"It wouldn't work. Not a sledgehammer or explosives. Not with this kind of safe," he said. "Now do what you're told. Open it."

She held up her bound wrists, figuring she had no choice but to go along with what he said until she figured out a plan B.

"How long have I been here?" she asked.

Baxter nodded toward the creep.

He looked at his wristwatch. "You slept around eleven hours."

That explained the hunger pangs. She'd been starved as a child at one of her foster homes. Mrs. Saint had used starvation tactics as punishment if the carpets hadn't been vacuumed when she got home from bridge club.

Eleven hours. That would make this Monday. Afternoon. Her brain cramped at trying to think. She was still woozy and more than a little bit nauseous.

Creep walked toward her with an opened blade from a pocketknife.

She sucked in a burst of air when he ran the blade alongside her cheek with a sneer.

"Just get it over with if you're going to kill me," she said through clenched teeth.

"Quit messing with her. Let's see what she knows, Landry," Baxter interjected.

"I haven't seen this thing since I was eighteen years old," she said. "I'm sure my father has changed the combination since then."

"Now we're getting somewhere," Baxter said, acknowledging that she'd just modified her recollection.

Again, he would only give her information if he planned to make sure she'd never sit across from him in a witness box. She thought about Tonto and her heart seized.

The creep sliced through the masking tape binding her wrists.

She motioned toward her ankles.

"I die and you'll go to prison for the rest of your life for the murder. Law enforcement is looking for me. They know who you are and that you've been chasing me around the country," she said to Baxter, looking him straight in the eye. She figured that she might as well play her cards, considering she had precious few.

"Are you threatening me?" He laughed but then his face twisted into a sneer. He nodded to the creep.

The creep picked up a backpack before sliding on a pair of plastic gloves. He pulled a rope with a hangman's knot tied to it. He tugged at the noose.

Baxter took a menacing step toward her. "It's terrible what happened to that girl from Hatch. It was her turbulent upbringing that caused her to turn on the two people who'd rescued her from the system. The only people who loved her and provided her with a home, food and clothing, according to interested neighbors."

Baxter let out a wicked-sounding squeal. The man was psycho.

"No one will believe you. I loved Randy and Julie Bristol. People will testify to that effect," she countered.

"No one's saying that you didn't love your foster parents. It's precisely your love for them and subsequent betrayal that caused the guilt to drive you crazy. You couldn't live with yourself anymore. So... pity really...you hung yourself." Baxter physically punctuated his sentence by pretending to place the noose around his neck and pulling. He let his eyes bulge and stuck his tongue out, mimicking a dead person hanging from a rope.

He walked to her, stopping in front of her and then ran his finger along her jawline.

"A shame to waste such a pretty girl."

"You can't make me put that thing around my neck." She breathed steady breaths to hold on to tendrils of what little calm she could.

"That's where you're wrong," Baxter said. "I can do anything I want."

Deputy Talisman.

"Law enforcement knows that you have a deputy

in your pocket. The FBI is being brought in to investigate Talisman," she lied. She had no idea how it would work and prayed that Baxter had none, either.

The look that flashed across his face was priceless.

She tried to work the bindings on her feet as discreetly as possible. At least her hands were free. Was there any way she could get to her feet and charge toward the creep? Have a go at his weapon?

Her legs were numb and she couldn't remember the last time she felt anything other than prickly sensations on her feet. Without blood circulation she didn't stand much of a chance of carrying out her plan.

The thought that her twins might find a news story someday that said their mother had taken her own life heated her blood to boiling.

In the shed, it was two against one, and she already knew the creep was strong. She'd picked up a few martial-arts skills but they were mostly defensive maneuvers.

Baxter grabbed her by the back of her hair and pulled her off the ground a few inches. Her hands came up and grabbed hold of his hands.

She used momentum to twist her body around while gripping his hands and land a kick to his groin. He grunted.

"Bitch," Baxter screamed.

He doubled over. She rolled onto her back and thrust her feet toward his head.

Chapter Eighteen

"So, let me make sure I'm understanding this correctly…" Mitch was done being patient. He and Zach had been riding shotgun in separate cruisers with well-meaning deputies for—he glanced at the clock—eleven hours straight.

The most productive thing about their meeting up at the gas station so far was the caffeine. Mitch had downed his first cup and was on his second. Adrenaline was wearing thin and he needed the boost. "We're no closer to figuring out where she could be, and all we're planning to do about it is drive around some more and hope we stumble across Baxter or where his goons may have taken Kimberly?"

"Everyone in the county is looking for her. Hell, everyone in the state," Zach stated. "You have a small fleet of airplanes in the air. If you can think of a better course of action, I'd like to hear it."

His cousin was just as frustrated as he was. Mitch could tell based on the stress cracks on his forehead.

There was no sign of Kimberly. No sightings.

Deputy Talisman was being interrogated. So far, to no avail.

Her cell phone had been dumped on the side of the highway outside El Paso. She had to be right under their noses and they were missing it.

"You're the one with law-enforcement experience. What does your gut tell you?" Mitch asked his cousin. He wasn't trying to frustrate Zach; he just wanted Kimberly home safely where she belonged.

"That she's here and we're missing something," he said.

"Is she still alive? Wait. Don't answer that." Mitch changed his mind. He didn't want to hear statistics. She *had* to be alive. He couldn't accept another outcome. "We're looking for a needle in a haystack."

"I know it seems that way," Zach began.

Mitch issued a sharp sigh. Eleven hours had passed. He checked his watch. Eleven hours and fifteen minutes to be exact. He couldn't allow himself to go to a place in his mind where this ended badly. There was too much left unsaid between him and Kimberly, dammit.

Deputy Bright walked up to the pair. He glanced at Mitch. "Ready?"

Mitch nodded before thanking the man. It couldn't be much fun for him to have Mitch riding along for his twelve-hour shift. Speaking of which, a shift change would come up soon. Mitch wondered how long the sheriff would be able to allocate his resources to one case without any leads.

It was a short walk to the cruiser.

As he gripped the handle, Zach called out.

Mitch turned in time to see Zach waving him over. His cell was to his ear. A knot twisted in his gut as he hightailed it over to his cousin.

"Where is that?" Zach asked the caller as he made eye contact with Mitch. The call was on speaker and Deputy Stillwater nodded. Stillwater was tall, dark in complexion and had an athletic build. He wore a white Stetson and reflective sunglasses. He had a serious expression and looked like the kind of guy who wouldn't put up with a lot of flak.

"I know that location," Stillwater said. "It used to be named Shoots but it's been closed a few years."

"He's sure?" Zach said into the receiver after a nod of acknowledgment to the deputy.

"We've already sent people to watch Baxter's home and other known hangouts. There's been no activity, sir," the female voice assured. "We're out of ideas. Talisman started talking a few minutes ago. I ran out of the room to call you."

No activity at Baxter's local haunts for hours on end sounded odd even to a civilian. But Talisman's giving up the location could be a trap. Even if Baxter was there, he could've been alerted.

Not that Mitch and Zach had another option.

"We're on our way," Zach confirmed with a look toward Stillwater. The deputy nodded.

Deputy Bright was already making tracks to his vehicle. Mitch took off running to catch up.

Hope was a slippery slope, so he wouldn't go down that path just yet.

"Where are we going and how far away is Shoots?" he asked Bright.

"About twenty minutes," Bright replied, pushing buttons to turn on the lights and siren. Wheels spewed gravel as they peeled out of the parking lot. "We'll go dark as soon as we get closer."

Mitch had a feeling this was going to be the longest twenty minutes of his life.

Five minutes out, Bright darkened the lights and turned off the siren. A ride that was supposed to take twenty minutes took sixteen at the speeds he traveled.

He and Bright were the first to arrive to the location, almost immediately followed by Zach and Stillwater. The place was still set up as an outdoor shooting range.

Mitch shouldered the door open. He recognized a couple of trap fields and more than double that in skeet fields.

"Hold on," Bright said. "I need you to stay in the vehicle."

As much as Mitch had no plans to get in the way of law enforcement, he couldn't sit idly by.

"I won't interfere," he promised.

Bright issued a sharp sigh. "Sir, I can't allow—"

Stillwater and Zach were already out of their vehicle.

"I take full responsibility for him," Zach said.

"With all due respect you're out of your jurisdiction, Sheriff," Bright said. "Protocol's in place for a reason."

"I'd like to offer my assistance as backup. I'm a sworn peace officer and you need all the help you can get," Zach continued.

Time was wasting.

"We can't afford to lose another minute. We'll stay right here. Just find her and bring her back alive," Mitch said.

Stillwater called for backup. He and Bright had their weapons out, sweeping from side to side as they moved, methodically clearing obstacles and small makeshift buildings.

"So we just stand here?" Mitch asked Zach.

A plane flew overhead. And then another.

"We need to find cover. Standing out here like this, we're an easy target. Baxter or one of his men could come out from behind one of these obstacles, shooting," Zach said.

"How do we know he's here?" Mitch asked, following Zach around a barricade, where they crouched low. The sun was high in the sky, heat bearing down on them.

"I overhead a report that two vehicles were parked near a shed on the property," Zach answered.

"This person say anything about seeing her?" Mitch asked.

Zach shook his head. Mitch didn't want to think about the fact that this could be a wild-goose chase.

That Kimberly could have been murdered hours ago and left in a ditch along the highway or, like Tonto, tossed out of the back of a vehicle...

His cousin had his phone out and he was studying a map. "Follow me."

"Where to?" Zach was too smart to get them mixed up in friendly fire.

"We need to locate the vehicles. If things go sour Baxter will use his SUV to flee the scene."

Smart.

Zach pulled out his Glock and led the way with it.

"You have a spare one of those?" Mitch didn't like the idea of being the only one showing up to the party unarmed.

"This didn't come from me." Zach reached down to his ankle holster and retrieved a pistol.

Mitch accepted the offering, thanked him and then followed his cousin.

Beads of sweat rolled down Mitch's face in the dry, blistering New Mexico heat as they progressed toward the location.

Rapid shots fired, crackling like fireworks, freezing them in their tracks. Both dropped to the ground and then rolled onto their stomachs.

"Stay low," Zach whispered as they belly crawled toward an expensive-looking white SUV. Parked next to it was a late-model king-cab pickup truck. "They come out this way and we've got 'em."

Mitch knew enough about gun safety to realize he needed to put a solid barrier between the two of them and whoever came at them. He scanned the area and located a three-and-a-half-foot-tall concrete wall. It was approximately five feet wide. No doubt another tool meant for training Baxter's lackeys.

A small measure of hope tried to take root at the fact that the men hadn't been shooting Kimberly to kill. But then again all that really said was they needed her for something.

Once they got it, she'd most likely be tossed aside just like Tonto.

Again, Mitch couldn't allow the possibility to take seed in his thoughts. In order to push ahead he had to be convinced that she was still alive.

More bullets split the air. Zach muttered a few choice words as he palmed his cell. He fired off a text asking for an update from the sheriff and then stared at the screen.

He muttered another curse.

"We can't go in blind," Zach said. "We could end up hurting more than helping."

"I can't imagine how that could be possible," Mitch countered. A shot of adrenaline made it even harder to sit back and wait. Do nothing. The sound of blood rushing in his ears matched the *thump-thump-thump* of his heartbeat. The only good news so far was that Baxter was on-site.

Mitch didn't want to consider the possibility that Kimberly had been taken somewhere else. All signs pointed to her being here.

"This is hell for me, too," Zach admitted. He glanced at his screen again. "Nothing yet. It'll come."

Those last two words sounded more like hope than promise.

And then Zach's phone vibrated.

He put it on speaker and turned the volume down so low that Mitch could scarcely hear.

"I have two men down on the scene. ETA for backup is twenty-three minutes," Sheriff Knell said, sounding solemn. "Do not engage with the suspect. I repeat. Do not engage."

Zach's expression wore the stress cracks of a seasoned soldier returning from battle. Mitch had spent enough time around law enforcement to realize no one wanted to leave men down if they could help.

"What are the numbers?" Zach asked.

"Two men holed up in a shed," Sheriff Knell reported.

"Any signs of a female victim?"

"My officers have no idea if anyone else is inside that shed." The sheriff's voice was heavy.

Zach thanked his colleague and ended the call. He stared at Mitch. "You heard the man. We have no idea if she's in there."

"She is." Mitch couldn't say why he knew but a sense of certainty came over him. "Why else would they shoot if they had nothing to hide?"

"There are a lot of reasons. This could be the home base of their operation," he said.

Mitch examined his cousin. He could get a read on him with one look.

"That's not what you really believe," Mitch said.

"Good men are out there, dying. I'm going in one way or another. I'm just trying to figure out a way to keep you out of this," Zach said honestly.

"Then there's no reason to waste another minute sitting here." Mitch hopped to his feet.

"First instinct will be to go to the injured men. We need to secure the perimeter first. Baxter might be on the move. Best case is that he's still in the shed, figuring out his next step." Zach shot a look.

Mitch acknowledged that was the best scenario for the injured men. Not necessarily for Kimberly.

First things first, they needed to assess the situation up close.

"I won't do anything stupid."

"Didn't think you would," Zach replied as he crouched low and proceeded toward the trail.

Mitch followed, thighs burning as they passed the final barricade that lead to an open space about the size of an acre.

The trail opened up to flat land. A ten-by-twelve shed stood toward the right-hand side of the property. A ring of man-made barricades surrounded the area, making it easy for someone to navigate an escape situation.

Everything was still and dead quiet. There was no breeze. The sun pelted him, causing sweat to roll down the sides of his face.

Mitch scanned the area for signs of the officers. Two metal barrels to his left had fresh-looking blood streaks marking them. He nudged Zach and nodded toward the barrels.

Zach followed his gaze. He rocked his head slightly. His gaze swept the perimeter. The metal door to the shed was closed. There were no windows.

On closer inspection Mitch noticed a round cutout in place of a knob. The opening was large enough to fit a barrel and for someone to see through.

His cousin was eyeing the same area.

Zach turned to Mitch and signaled that he was going to check on the deputies. Another signal from his cousin indicated that he wanted Mitch to cover him.

Zach doubled back the way they came. Smart.

Zach reappeared in Mitch's sightline at the double barrels. The next thing he saw was his cousin administering CPR from behind the barrels.

Mitch kept vigilant watch at the metal door.

It swung open and his heart cramped.

Kimberly stumbled out and took a few unsteady steps.

His heart clutched.

"Don't shoot," she pleaded, dropping to her knees.

A clean-cut man stepped behind her and forced her to stand. Her body blocked a clean shot.

From the corner of his eye, he saw Zach abandon CPR and pop to his feet, crouching low behind the barrels. He wouldn't do anything stupid.

The barrel of a gun poked out of the hole on the shed's door.

Mitch had no way to warn Zach and could only hope that his cousin could see it.

And then he realized what was about to happen.

Baxter sidestepped as the shot cracked the air.

Kimberly's eyes widened as she searched her body. A red dot flowered on her stomach. Mitch had to stop himself from going nuts, giving away his location and getting himself killed. As much as he wanted to run toward her, he realized that's exactly what the men wanted. He refused to play into their hands.

Baxter took off a second later to Mitch's right, an easier trail to his SUV.

Fighting the urge to run to Kimberly, Mitch darted after Baxter instead.

The next thing he knew, Baxter had spun around on him and drawn a weapon. Before the man could get off a shot, Mitch fired.

Gunning toward Baxter at full speed, Mitch experienced a rush of adrenaline that made it impossible for him to steady his hand, but he was close enough for the bullet to take a chunk out of the inside of Baxter's left arm.

Baxter instinctively grabbed his wound.

Mitch took another couple of steps and then dove headfirst into the man's knees, knocking him backward and causing him to lose his balance. He stumbled a step before falling. The gun in his right hand flew onto the hard, unforgiving earth a few feet away.

Baxter stretched toward the weapon but Mitch was already on top of him, connecting jabs to his jaw. Baxter's head jerked with every punch landed. Blood splattered everywhere, both from Baxter's nose and from Mitch's knuckles.

The sounds of more shots being fired behind him registered. The knot braiding Mitch's gut twisted relentlessly.

He nailed punch after punch until Baxter's body went limp underneath him.

Chapter Nineteen

The next thing Mitch knew he was being dragged off Baxter by two sets of hands that felt like vise grips around his arms.

It took a second to register that one of the voices shouting at him was his cousin's.

"Kimberly needs you," Zach said in an urgent tone.

Mitch stopped resisting and popped to his feet.

Zach stepped over Baxter's bloody frame.

"Patch him up," he said to one of the EMTs. "He's going to spend the rest of his life in jail. I want him well enough to serve his sentence for a very long lifetime."

Law enforcement had descended on the scene that was now a bustle of activity. EMTs were on the ground, working on someone—Kimberly.

Mitch bolted toward them, toward her.

"Let him through," Zach commanded, using the authoritative voice all lawmen seemed to possess.

Mitch dropped to his knees beside her as an EMT

allowed passage. He was performing chest compressions on her.

An oxygen mask covered most of her face. Seeing Kimberly lying there, lifeless, Mitch couldn't breathe.

He'd lost her once. He'd never survive losing her again and especially now that he knew the real her. Smart. Brave. Fierce.

Tears welled in his eyes. He swiped at them.

"Stay with me, Kimberly," he said, taking her by the hand. "Don't go away again. My life means nothing without you. I love you. I want you to stay here with me and our twins. Aaron and Rea need you. I need you."

There was no response from her still, breathless body.

This wasn't right. None of this was right.

Dammit.

He leaned down next to her ear.

"Can you hear me? These next words that I'm about to say never came easy to me before I met you. I love you. I need you. I'm half a man without you." He sniffed the tears that had started rolling down his nose.

And then her hand twitched.

He heard an EMT say, "She's breathing."

And another, "You're doing great. Chopper's landing. We're going to fix you right up."

The sudden bursts of wind and *chop-chop-chop*

of the helicopter registered somewhere in the back of Mitch's mind.

"Sir, we're taking her to Hope Memorial Hospital. Someone will take you there to meet us," the younger EMT said.

"Take good care of her," Mitch said.

Zach was already behind him, urging him toward the parking area. He glanced back to see that law-enforcement officers had the other one of Baxter's associates facedown and cuffed.

Kimberly's nightmare was over.

His was just beginning.

For three long days, Mitch held vigil by his wife's side after surgery to remove bullet fragments from her stomach. She'd been in and out of consciousness since then. Mostly out. The nurse had told him that she wouldn't remember any of this. Her vitals were strong. She was young and healthy. All signs pointed toward a full recovery. But no one knew for certain if she'd lost too much blood. Or if she'd ever be the same after the shooting.

His family had been taking shifts to keep him company. His brothers were at a hotel with Joyce and the twins. Amy and his sister, Amber, had gone to pick up an important package at the airport.

Exhaustion was wearing thin as Mitch sipped his umpteenth cup of coffee in the last seventy-two hours.

He watched his wife sleep, occasionally offering

words of reassurance. She was going to be fine. She *had* to be okay when she woke.

Mitch wasn't much of a praying man, but he wasn't afraid to admit that he'd called in a man of the cloth to pray over her. He figured it couldn't hurt.

His brothers made sure he got fresh coffee, and Joyce made him a homemade meal every day. He didn't want to insult her but he had no appetite. One of his brothers would cover for him, slipping out with a full plate and returning with an empty one.

"Come on, Kimberly," he finally said, wishing he could see those beautiful eyes of hers again.

And then Kimberly coughed. Her eyes opened. She blinked a few times as her eyes adjusted to the sunlight bathing the room.

"I can close the blinds," Mitch offered. His heart galloped.

Her eyes found him and his chest squeezed. There was nothing left of him to protect. The past seventy-two hours of not knowing if she'd ever wake had hollowed him out. Every encouraging sign that she was recovering meant nothing if he couldn't share his life with her.

"It's okay," she rasped.

She seemed to realize he was holding her hand. Her other one came up and searched around her neck.

"Are you looking for this?" He pulled her wedding ring still attached to a string out of his pocket. The nurse had given it to him for safekeeping before wheeling her into surgery.

Her eyes lit up when she saw the gold band. "Yes."

"I can get the nurse." He placed the makeshift necklace into her palm.

"No. Not yet. What happened?" She glanced around, looking a little scared.

"You're recovering from surgery," he said. "Baxter and his cronies are locked away. It's over. You're safe now."

Relief crossed her tense features.

"What day is it?" She tried to sit up.

"Hold on. Doc says you have to take it easy." He picked up a remote and placed it in her hand.

"I liked holding your hand better," she admitted and her cheeks flushed. It was the first sign of color in her face.

"You have no idea how happy it makes me to hear that."

"What time is it?" she asked, raising her bed to an upright position. Her voice cracked when she spoke.

Mitch checked his phone. "Four thirty."

He scooted the tray table next to her and brought a cup of water to her lips.

She took a sip. "That's good. My throat is so dry."

Hearing her voice and seeing her sit up were about the best things he'd ever experienced after fearing that he'd lost her.

"It's Thursday," he stated.

A look of confusion drew her brows together before she started counting on her fingers.

"I've been here for three days?"

"Surgery went well and you've been sleeping a lot," he said.

"Have you been here this whole time?" She didn't hide her shock at the revelation.

"Yes. And I'll be here for the rest of your life if you say the word." He dropped down beside her bed, took her hand in his and rested it against his forehead. He feared he'd overwhelm her with his next words but his heart was about to burst if he didn't say them. So he lifted his chin to look directly at her. "I love you, Kimberly. And I want my wife back home where she belongs, where *you* belong. What do you think? Will you come home with me?"

Tears streamed down her cheeks and she smiled the biggest smile he'd ever seen.

"I love you, Mitch. I can't wait to come home."

He stood up and pressed a tender kiss to her lips.

"How soon can I get out of here?" she asked. The spark in her eyes had returned.

A soft knock sounded at the door.

"Come in," Mitch said.

Zach peeked around the half-opened door. "Is this a good time?"

"Yes," Kimberly said with another smile.

Mitch and Zach exchanged bear hugs before Zach moved to Kimberly's side.

She motioned for Mitch to sit on the edge of the bed, which he did.

"I remember a couple of deputies being shot at. Are they here?" she asked.

Mitch hadn't had time to give her the bad news.

Zach tucked his chin to his chest in reverence. "We lost one. The other has been treated and released."

"Zach couldn't save them both," Mitch added. His cousin had done everything he could. Stillwater had survived because of Zach's quick thinking.

"I'm so sorry," Kimberly said.

Mitch had set up a fund to take care of Bright's parents. The loss of the young deputy had hit the community hard. Mitch had also set up a college scholarship fund in Bright's name in order to honor his memory.

"Baxter and his men will do hard time," Zach reassured. "It won't bring him back or take away the pain you've suffered. But justice will be served. Talisman will spend the rest of his life behind bars, too. He started talking as soon as he realized he was in a no-win situation."

"And did he say how my father was involved in all of this?" she asked.

"Tonto was desperate to get his sick grandmother across the border, where she could get medical care. He was introduced to Baxter, who promised to help if Tonto could get access to a van," Zach informed her. "That's when Tonto went to your father, who agreed to help. But then—"

"My father figured out the partnership between Deputy Talisman and Paul Baxter," she said on a sharp sigh.

"He had proof in the safe," Zach continued.

"That's what he was really talking about," she said.

Mitch's cell vibrated. He checked the screen and turned to Zach. "Mind keeping her company for a second?"

"Not at all." Zach took the seat next to Kimberly. "We can't replace the Bristols. I know you loved them very much. But you have family to lean on now. You'll never be alone again."

Mitch heard Kimberly sniff back tears as he stepped into the hallway.

The trio of women coming toward him wore the second biggest smiles he'd seen all day.

The one in the middle's resemblance to his wife caused him to perform a double take. Her hair was more brown than black—Kimberly's original color—and her nose was slightly bigger. But he didn't need an introduction.

"She doesn't know you're here," he said to Rose.

"I can't wait to see her. It's been so long," the younger version of Kimberly had tearstained cheeks. And when he really looked at them, so did Amy and Amber.

He thanked them both for delivering the "package" that had taken Isaac exactly six hours to track down. He'd been begging for work to do since he'd been released from the hospital and the incident with the heifer seemed to be isolated.

The first conversation had lasted three hours.

Rose had wanted to know everything about her older sister.

"I have goose bumps," Rose admitted. "I've thought about her every day for more years than I care to count."

"Well, then let's not keep you waiting any longer," Mitch said.

He stepped inside the door and then stepped to the side.

"There's someone here to see you," he said to Kimberly.

"The babies?" She perked up.

They would come a little later after being fed dinner. "Not exactly."

He nodded to Rose, who rushed in and to Kimberly's side.

Kimberly gasped and her hand covered her mouth. "It can't be. Is it really you?"

"It's me. Your little sister."

"You're okay," Kimberly said, throwing out her arms.

"Yeah." Rose seemed surprised. "I always had you with me to protect me."

She pulled out the charm on a string that Kimberly had given her before she'd been hauled off to a new home.

Tears streamed down Kimberly's cheeks as she pulled her sister into a hug.

Mitch took a back seat, chatting with his cousins and sister until the nurse came in, followed shortly by the doctor. The news was good. Kimberly was healing well and could leave the hospital in a couple of days.

The early evening hours flew by. Rose and Kimberly seemed to catch up on years in the span of a few hours.

A nurse came in and cleared everyone out, saying they could return once Kimberly ate her dinner and had a bath.

Mitch wrangled a spot in the chair next to his wife. Nothing and no one was going to keep the two of them apart again, and the nurse seemed to realize this as she excused herself to let Kimberly eat in peace. She promised to return in half an hour to help Kimberly bathe.

When the room was quiet and it was just the two of them again, Kimberly leaned toward Mitch.

"First you gave me love and then a family. Now my sister." Tears fell and he thumbed them away for her. "I'm a leaky faucet. But I just want to say that I can't imagine spending my life with a better man. I love you, Mitch Kent."

"The day we met is the day I found home," he said. "I'm ready to put the past behind us and start forever as a real family. No more hiding. No secrets. Just the two of us and our babies."

Kimberly wiped away more of those tears. "I love you. And I can't wait to go home."

* * * * *

Look for the next book in USA TODAY
bestselling author Barb Han's
Rushing Creek Crime Spree miniseries,
Ransom at Christmas,
available next month from
Harlequin Intrigue!

COMING NEXT MONTH FROM

⊞ HARLEQUIN®

INTRIGUE

Available October 22, 2019

#1887 ENEMY INFILTRATION
Red, White and Built: Delta Force Deliverance • by Carol Ericson
Horse trainer Lana Moreno refuses to believe her brother died during an
attack on the embassy outpost he was guarding. Her last hope to uncover
the truth is Delta Force soldier Logan Hess, who has his own suspicions
about the attack. Can they survive long enough to discover what happened?

#1888 RANSOM AT CHRISTMAS
Rushing Creek Crime Spree • by Barb Han
Kelly Morgan has been drugged, and the only thing she can remember
is that she's in danger. When rancher Will Kent finds her on his ranch, he
immediately takes her to safety, putting himself in the sights of a murderer
in the process.

#1889 SNOWBLIND JUSTICE
Eagle Mountain Murder Mystery: Winter Storm Wedding
by Cindi Myers
Brodie Langtry, an investigator with the Colorado Bureau of Investigation, is
in town to help with the hunt for the Ice Cold Killer. He's shocked when he
discovers that Emily Walker, whom he hasn't seen in years, is the murderer's
next target.

#1890 WARNING SHOT
Protectors at Heart • by Jenna Kernan
Sheriff Axel Trace is not sure Homeland Security agent Rylee Hockings's
presence will help him keep the peace in his county. But when evidence
indicates that a local terrorist group plans to transport a virus over the
US-Canadian border, the two must set aside their differences to save their
country.

#1891 RULES IN DECEIT
Blackhawk Security • by Nichole Severn
Network analyst Elizabeth Dawson thought she'd moved on from the
betrayal that destroyed her career—that is, until Braxton Levitt shows up one
day claiming there's a target on her back only he can protect her against.

#1892 WITNESS IN THE WOODS
by Michele Hauf
Conservation officer Joe Cash protects all kinds of endangered creatures,
but the stakes have never been higher. Now small-animal vet Skylar Davis
is seeking Joe's protection after being targeted by the very poachers he's
investigating.

———————

HICNM1019

"Let's try this again." Logan wiped his dusty palm against his
shirt and held out his hand. "I'm Captain Logan Hess with US
Delta Force."

Her mouth formed an O but at least she took his hand this time
in a firm grip, her skin rough against his. "I'm Lana Moreno, but
you probably already know that, don't you?"

"I sure do." He jerked his thumb over his shoulder. "I saw
your little impromptu news conference about an hour ago."

"But you knew who I was before that. You didn't track me
down to compare cowboy boots." She jabbed him in the chest
with her finger. "Did you know Gilbert?"

"Unfortunately, no." Lana didn't need to know just how
unfortunate that really was. "Let's get out of the dirt and grab
some lunch."

She tilted her head and a swathe of dark hair fell over her
shoulder, covering one eye. The other eye scorched his face.
"Why should I have lunch with you? What do you want from

me? When I heard you were Delta Force, I thought you might have known Gilbert, might've known what happened at that outpost."

"I didn't, but I know of Gilbert and the rest of them, even the assistant ambassador who was at the outpost. I can guarantee I know a lot more about the entire situation than you do from reading that redacted report they grudgingly shared with you."

"You are up-to-date. What are we waiting for?" Her feet scrambled beneath her as she slid up the wall. "If you have any information about the attack in Nigeria, I want to hear it."

"I thought you might." He rose from the ground, towering over her petite frame. He pulled a handkerchief from the inside pocket of his leather jacket and waved it at her. "Take this."

"Thank you." She blew her nose and mopped her face, running a corner of the cloth beneath each eye to clean up her makeup. "I suppose you don't want it back."

"You can wash it for me and return it the next time we meet."

That statement earned him a hard glance from those dark eyes, still sparkling with unshed tears, but he had every intention of seeing Lana Moreno again and again—however many times it took to pick her brain about why she believed there was more to the story than a bunch of Nigerian criminals deciding to attack an embassy outpost. It was a ridiculous cover story if he ever heard one.

About as ridiculous as the story of Major Rex Denver working with terrorists.

Her quest had to be motivated by more than grief over a brother. People didn't stage stunts like she just did in front of a congressman's office based on nothing.

Don't miss
Enemy Infiltration *by Carol Ericson,*
available November 2019 wherever
Harlequin® Intrigue *books and ebooks are sold.*

www.Harlequin.com